DINOSAURS ON OTHER PLANETS

DINOSAURS ON OTHER PLANETS

STORIES

DANIELLE McLAUGHLIN

RANDOM HOUSE
NEW YORK

Copyright © 2016 by Danielle McLaughlin

All rights reserved.

Published in the United States by Random House, an imprint and division of Penguin Random House LLC, New York.

RANDOM HOUSE and the HOUSE colophon are registered trademarks of Penguin Random House LLC.

The following stories were originally published in *The New Yorker:* "Dinosaurs on Other Planets" (originally published as "The Dinosaurs on Other Planets") (September 15, 2014) and "In the Act of Falling" (September 7, 2015).

LIBRARY OF CONGRESS CATALOGING-IN-PUBLICATION DATA
McLaughlin, Danielle
[Short stories. Selections]
Dinosaurs on other planets: stories / Danielle McLaughlin.
pages cm
ISBN 978-0-8129-9842-9
ebook ISBN 978-0-8129-9843-6
I. Title.
PR6113.C523A6 2016
823'.92—dc23
2015026648

Printed in the United States of America on acid-free paper

randomhousebooks.com

2 4 6 8 9 7 5 3 1

First Edition

Book design by Susan Turner

CONTENTS

THE ART OF FOOT-BINDING   3

THOSE THAT I FIGHT I DO NOT HATE   27

ALL ABOUT ALICE   39

ALONG THE HERON-STUDDED RIVER   51

NIGHT OF THE SILVER FOX   71

NOT OLEANDERS   91

SILHOUETTE   113

A DIFFERENT COUNTRY   133

THE SMELL OF DEAD FLOWERS   153

IN THE ACT OF FALLING   185

DINOSAURS ON OTHER PLANETS   209

ACKNOWLEDGMENTS   239

DINOSAURS ON OTHER PLANETS

THE ART OF FOOT-BINDING

---

*Begin on the feast day of the goddess Guanyin, that she
may grant mercy. Or on the cusp of winter when the cold
will numb bones splintered like ice on a broken lake. Begin
when she is young, when the bones are closer to water
and a foot may be altered like the course of a mountain
stream.*

IT IS TUESDAY AND THE WOMAN WHO COMES TO CLEAN
has been in, leaving the hall smelling like the inside of a
taxi, a synthetic pine fragrance called Alpine Spring, though
it is the first week of November. Janice unbuttons her wet
coat, hangs it on a peg. She has thought to mention that
she dislikes the scent, but she and the cleaner rarely over-
lap, and, written down—*I do not like the air freshener*—the
complaint seems trivial, almost petty. There is also the fact

that the woman cleans for a number of other mothers at the school. Janice already senses a hierarchy of allegiances, suspects minor betrayals and indiscretions.

Music is coming from upstairs, a heavy thud of bass that vibrates through the ceiling: the sound of Becky skipping hockey practice. Mrs. Harding from next door will be around. She will have been sitting by her front window, watching for Janice's return, and will now be struggling into her ankle-length fur, lacing up her shoes, ready for the assault on Janice's front steps. She will complain how the wet leaves make them slippery, as if Janice has set a trap, and then, the music stopped, she will sit for an hour at the kitchen table, sniffing a cup of tea and talking.

As she climbs the stairs, Janice pauses on the half landing to rearrange the collection of crystals, miniature figurines of birds and animals. They are displayed on a table by the window where the light shows them to best advantage. Every Tuesday, the cleaner removes them to dust the table, and every Tuesday returns them in reverse order. Today, inexplicably, the table appears not to have been dusted, and still they are out of position.

In her daughter's bedroom, a row of stuffed toys gazes from a shelf. The years haven't been kind, each toy suffering its own peculiar disability: a ragged tailless Eeyore, a molting one-eyed teddy bear. Becky scowls when she sees her mother. "I told you to knock," she says, switching off the music. She turned fourteen the previous July, and has suddenly grown taller and broader. Her face, already too round to be pretty, has become rounder, and she has taken to wearing her long brown hair, her best feature, in a tight bun. She is sitting on the bed, still in her school blouse and skirt. Her shoes and her gray woolen socks have been removed, and she is winding a pair of Janice's tights around her right foot, the nylon already laddered where it stretches across her toes.

"What do you think you're doing?" Janice says.

"Binding my feet."

Janice watches her daughter attempt to curl her toes underneath her foot, watches them spring back up again. "You're kidding, right?"

"It's for a history project with Ms. Matthews. Basically, it's about how women suffered long ago."

"I still don't understand why you're binding your feet."

"So I can em-pa-thize?" Becky says. "So I can see what it was like to be oppressed? Basically."

"How old is Ms. Matthews?"

Becky doesn't answer. She is winding the tights in a band around her toes. Just below her ankle is a silvery pink scar where she caught it in a door as a child, and the skin has grown back a shade lighter. She takes a strip of white material from a pile beside her on the bed and begins bandaging her foot, winding the cloth round and round, until the foot is a white stub.

Split the belly of a live calf and place her feet in the wound, deep, so that blood covers the ankles. If there is no calf,

*heat the blood of a monkey until it boils. Add mulberry
root and tannin. Soak the feet until the skin is soft.*

THE ROOM IS COLD, and Janice makes her way across
the debris on the floor—underwear, magazines, aerosol
canisters—to close the window. Tampons in brightly colored
wrappers spill like sweets from a box on the dressing table,
beside eye shadows and lip gloss. They seem out of place,
these adult things, as if a child has been playing with the contents of her mother's handbag. The bedroom is toward the
back of the house and overlooks a narrow garden that slopes
to the river. When Becky was small, Janice had worried that
she would wander away and drown, and one summer Philip
constructed a fence from sheets of metal nailed to wooden
stakes. It has served its purpose but is an eyesore now, the
metal sheeting buckled and rusted. Once spring arrives, Janice thinks, once the days are longer and the weather milder,
she will dismantle it. She shuts the window and draws across
the curtains.

Becky is still busy with the tights. Beside her on the bed
are several sheets of paper, including one headed "The Art
of Foot-Binding," a poor-quality facsimile of a handwritten
manual. Next to it is a page of photos and diagrams, some
accompanied by instructions: *Rub the feet with bian stone,
or a piece of bull's horn.* Janice does not immediately recognize the thing in the photographs as a foot. It is a grayish-
white lump, toes melted into the sole like plastic that has

been left too near a fire. The owner of the foot smiles shyly out at the camera. There is something grotesque, almost sordid, in the way she displays her deformity, like a freak act from an old traveling circus, and Janice looks away, back to her daughter's feet. As she watches Becky winding the strips round and round, she recognizes the delicate scalloping of the Egyptian cotton pillowcases from the guest bedroom.

"Damn it, Becky! Have you any idea how much those cost? Couldn't you have used something else? Anything else?"

"I searched everywhere," Becky says. "There was nothing else. If you were home, I could've asked you for something else, but you weren't."

"Maybe I should explain to Ms. Matthews the oppressive cost of pillowcases."

Becky scowls, stops winding the bandages. "Why are you being such a bitch about Ms. Matthews?"

"Haven't I told you not to use that word?"

"What word?"

"You know what word. And for the record, I've no problem with Ms. Matthews. I just think she's got weird ideas about homework."

"You hate her," Becky says.

Janice takes a deep breath. "I don't hate her," she says slowly. "I've never even met her." But as she says it, she remembers, from the open house two years previously, a slight red-haired woman with a choppy asymmetrical hairstyle and Ugg boots, though she had thought of her then as a girl because she was barely distinguishable from the gaggle of teenagers flocking around her.

"If you'd gone to the parent-teacher meeting you'd have met her. Dad met her. Dad likes her."

Janice considers this, decides to let it go. She begins to pick up clothes from the floor and hang them in the wardrobe.

Becky continues bandaging her foot. "Ms. Roberts hates her, too," she says, "but Ms. Roberts is jealous because Ms. Matthews is a dote and everybody thinks Ms. Roberts is a cunt. Which she is, basically."

"Becky!" Janice stops gathering clothes. "You are never to say that word again. Do you hear me?"

"Ms. Matthews lets us say anything we like."

"I'm warning you, Becky. . . ." There comes then the sound she has been hoping for—the sound of the house phone ringing. "We're not finished with this, Becky," she says, wagging a finger at her daughter. "Not by a long shot."

When the skin is smooth, break the four small toes below the second joint and fold them underneath. Take a knife and peel away the nails. They may creep like Mongolian death worms into the darkness of the heel and that way a foot may be lost.

THE EVENING BEFORE, SHE had gone with Philip to a fortieth birthday party in a restaurant in Douglas village. Angela, the birthday girl, was an old college friend. More precisely, she was an old college friend of Philip's, because although they had all been part of the same set once, Janice had never liked her. Angela's three teenage daughters were there, afflicted already with their mother's mannerisms: the coy, flirtatious giggle, a tendency to stand too close and engage in unnecessary touching. They had rushed, shrieking, at Philip, and one of them, the middle one, had called him "uncle" and kissed him.

In the car on the way home, Janice said, "I think Angela's got too thin. It's showing in her face."

"I thought she looked well," he said. "She didn't look forty, that's for sure."

Janice was driving. She glanced at him in the passenger seat, but he was staring out the window. "Know what her sister told me?" she said. "Angela has them all on diets. Those poor girls. That little one can't be any more than twelve."

"Fourteen," he said. "Same age as Becky."

"That's still way too young, Philip."

"She's banned crisps and chocolate," he said, turning to her. "It's hardly a human rights issue."

They were approaching a junction and she braked sharply. "And that's what you and Angela were discussing?" she said. "Holed up together at the bar all night?"

He sighed. "Angela likes you," he said. "She's only ever tried to be a friend. I wish you'd give her a chance. We were talking about Becky, actually, about how she's put on weight."

"I don't believe this," she said.

"Come on," he said. "You must have noticed, too."

"I'll tell you what I noticed," she said. "You sweet-talking plastic Angela all night. If it wasn't Angela it was one of the daughters. Don't think I didn't see. That blond one had her hand practically on your ass at one stage. She's worse than her mother."

"Let me out," he said. "Let me out here. I'll walk home." They were stopped at traffic lights, and he rattled the car door but it was locked.

"Big fucking gesture, Philip—we must be a whole five minutes away." But she was crying, wiping her eyes furtively with the back of her hand. He could have reached across and released the lock, but he remained in his seat, and when the lights changed she drove on. He didn't speak again until they pulled up outside the house. She was sobbing now, tears running down her cheeks. He unfastened his seatbelt.

"Did you ever think our lives would turn out like this?" he said.

Prepare bandages of white silk or cotton, ten chi *long and two* cun *wide. Break the arch of the foot and wind the cloths in figures of eight, knotting at instep and ankle. Do not be unsettled by the cries: The breeze that sighs at night about the lotus bulb, by morning gives way to petaled sun.*

SHE HURRIES ACROSS THE landing to their bedroom and picks up the phone. "Hi," she says.

"Hi."

These postfight conversations have the quality of a folk dance, a complicated system of advance and retreat, executed with varying degrees of grace. Perform the correct movements, in the correct order, and eventually they will be returned to the point they departed from. "Listen," he says. "I shouldn't have said those things last night. I'm sorry."

"We were both tired," she says. "Angela always puts me on edge. I don't know why I let her get to me."

"Angela has a way of getting to people," he says. "It's her special talent." And she knows he doesn't mean it, knows he likes Angela, has possibly even fucked her at some point, but she understands, too, that he is offering Angela up by way of apology. She lies back on the bed and closes her eyes.

"I've been thinking," she says. "What you said last night, about Becky's weight? I'm going to have a word with her."

"Don't, please," he says. "I was out of order."

"No," she says. "You weren't." Mostly because it was expected, but now that she has said it aloud, she wonders if perhaps he mightn't be right.

"I'd hate her to be upset," he says. "She's a great kid. But whatever you think is best."

"It wouldn't do her any harm to lose a few pounds." She waits for him to say something else, but he falls silent. She senses he is preparing to wind down the call. "Will you be home for supper?" she asks, while she tries to think of something else to say, something to hold him.

"I'm afraid not. I have to take clients to dinner."

"Where will you take them?" she says, but already he is saying "bye, bye, bye," and then he is gone.

She returns the phone to its cradle and sits a moment on the edge of the bed. These calls usually act as a sort of poultice, the fact of them more than anything that might be said. This one was different. It was the way he hurried to say goodbye, she thinks, the way he managed to take leave of her so very easily. She goes to the mirror to fix her hair. Her hand flies to her throat when she sees Becky in the doorway. "Goodness, Becky!" she says. "You gave me a fright."

"Was that Dad on the phone?"

Janice nods. How long has the child been there? she wonders.

Becky begins rhythmically kicking the doorframe, five kicks with the right foot, five with the left, her feet encased in wads of white pillowcase. "Is he coming home for supper?"

"No, he's meeting clients." She points to the bandages on her daughter's feet. "Take those off and go do the rest of your homework."

Becky shakes her head. "No can do. I've only just put them on."

Janice goes over and tugs at a loose end of cloth on her daughter's right foot. The girl yells and kicks out, catching her mother on the wrist. She turns and heads in an odd, stumbling gait toward her own bedroom, arms held out from her sides as if negotiating a tightrope. One of the bandages comes loose, unfurling behind her as she walks.

Janice rubs her wrist. "That's it, Becky," she says, following her across the landing. "I'm going to the school tomorrow. I'm going to see Ms. Matthews."

Becky has reached the door of her own bedroom. "That's a coincidence," she says, "because Ms. Matthews wants to see you." She pulls a piece of paper from the pocket of her skirt and, crumpling it in a ball, flings it at her mother, striking her in the chest. Then she goes into her room, slams the door, and turns the lock.

Janice picks up the piece of paper, smooths it out. It is an appointment slip headed with the school's blue crest, the spaces for day and time left blank. A handwritten note in large, looped writing, little circles over the *i*'s, asks her to telephone to arrange an appointment. There is nothing else, no clue as to the nature of the meeting sought, only a signature in the same looped script: Madeleine Matthews. The slip is dated two days previously. Janice bangs on her daughter's door. "Becky," she says. "Why does Ms. Matthews want to see me?" But there is no answer. When she tries again—"You're being childish, Becky. We need to talk about this"—Becky still doesn't reply. But when Janice is halfway down the stairs, she thinks she hears her daughter say something, something that sounds very like "bitch."

If a foot is large, or the toes fleshy, place among the bandages shards of glass or porcelain. This will bring a rotting of flesh which, in time, will drop away, leaving the foot smaller and more pleasing. Bind at least twice a week, or,

if the family is rich, every day. Soon, a valley will form
between cleft and heel, dark and secret as a jade gate.

DOWNSTAIRS, SHE POURS A glass of wine and sits at the kitchen table. She thinks of Philip, in a restaurant somewhere, eating attractive food served by attractive waitresses with soft, glossy mouths. She shuts her eyes, but instead of disappearing, the waitresses come into clearer focus, a troupe of smiling, agreeable young women. And as the image sharpens it begins to morph, the women layered one on top of another, until they merge into one, a woman with red choppy hair, incongruously, for a restaurant, standing before a whiteboard. It is Ms. Matthews. Happy, unbroken Ms. Matthews, glowing with that singularly youthful emotion: hope. Oblivious Ms. Matthews, reaching back through the centuries to find herself a bit of trouble. And though Janice knows it is a trick of the mind, still it unsettles her.

There hasn't been another woman, at least none of any significance, since Mandy Wilson's mother six years ago; this she is reasonably sure of. There has, perhaps, been an occasional, discreet straying, evidenced by a temporary distancing when he gets home from a business trip, a restraint in the way he touches her. But nothing like that time when she feared she had lost him. Then, even the nights he was home, asleep beside her, she would get up and walk the house in the small hours, touching things, trailing her fingers along walls, the backs of chairs, as if trying to hold down whatever it was that was slipping away.

Other nights she had taken things out to the garden, things

singled out for destruction during the day: ornaments, serving dishes, a shell brought back from holiday. She would go to the end of the property, where Philip wouldn't hear, and she would smash them against the fence. One such night, glass littering the ground at her feet, she had looked back up the garden and had seen a light come on in the house next door, saw the blinds raised, the outline of Mrs. Harding's face at the window.

But she had endured somehow, and her endurance had been rewarded. He had come to his senses, as she knew he would, and when Becky's birthday came round, Janice had walked up to Mandy Wilson's mother at the school gates and handed her an invitation. Mandy's mother turned up at their house that Friday afternoon, her daughter shy beside her in a blue party dress. She accepted a glass of elderflower cordial, complimented the cut of the crystal. And then she and Janice and the other mothers had engaged in shrill, giddy conversation, had even laughed, if a little hysterically, while small girls ran up and down the stairs, or sat in circles on the floor, plaiting each other's hair.

Go before dawn to the statue of the Tiny-Footed Maiden. There you must leave balls of rice mixed with wolfberry, and a pair of silk slippers, no bigger than a sparrow.

THE SCHOOL COMPRISES THREE two-story blocks of 1970s buildings and a glass and steel extension that houses the computer labs. The school insignia, MATER MISERACORDIA, is in steel lettering above the entrance. Ms. Matthews is waiting for her in an empty classroom, correcting assignments at a long rectangular desk. Her hair covers her face as she bends over a copybook. A pack of coloring pencils, neatly pared, lies beside a pink stapler and a dish of multicolored paper clips. "You must be Becky's mum," she says, standing up to shake hands. "Janice, isn't it?"

"That's right," Janice says. She notices that Ms. Matthews doesn't say what she is to call her.

"Please," Ms. Matthews says, gesturing to a chair on the opposite side of the desk, and Janice sits down.

Ms. Matthews sits back in her own chair, and her hands erupt in a flurry of busyness. She moves the stapler an inch to the left, squares the edges of a sheaf of paper. Janice watches her run a finger along the inside collar of her blouse, adjusting it, though it already stands so rigid it may have been starched. "So," Ms. Matthews says, bringing her hands to rest on the desk in front of her. "You got my note."

"I wanted to see you anyway, as it happens."

"Oh?" Ms. Matthews's hand goes again to her collar, just a quick touch this time.

"Yes, it's about the foot-binding. I don't feel it's"—she pauses to allow the word more resonance—"appropriate."

Ms. Matthews's head tilts slightly to one side. "It's something I do with my girls every year. They usually find it interesting."

Her girls? Janice thinks. What proprietary claim can this woman possibly make, she who is barely more than a girl herself? And every year? How many years could that be, exactly? Three? Four?

"It's a bit medieval, isn't it?" Janice says. "Literally."

"Well, actually," Ms. Matthews says, "and this is very interesting, it was practiced in certain remote parts of China up until the 1940s. But it's not about the dates, is it? I prefer to take a broader sociological perspective." She has picked up a ballpoint pen and is striking it against the desk, not unlike something Becky might do, and Janice has to fight an urge to tell her to stop.

"They're fourteen," Janice says. "Their feet are still growing, it could damage their bones."

Ms. Matthews frowns. "Sorry?" she says. "I'm not following—"

"I've seen how tightly Becky winds those bandages. It could cut off circulation."

Ms. Matthews edges her chair back, putting a fraction more distance between herself and Janice. "Obviously," she says, "we don't do any actual foot-binding. Basically, we discuss it, watch videos on YouTube, that sort of thing."

The classroom feels suddenly hot and airless. Janice wants to open a window, but Ms. Matthews is speaking. "Perhaps," she is saying, "this brings us, in a roundabout way, to why I wanted to see you. Have you noticed Becky seems unsettled lately, more withdrawn than usual?"

Than usual? And is Becky withdrawn? Quiet, certainly, but "withdrawn" is different, isn't it? "Withdrawn" is something else. "She's a teenager," Janice says. "'Withdrawn' is the factory setting," and she hates herself as soon as she's said it.

"As you know," Ms. Matthews says, "Becky finds school socially challenging. That's always been a problem, but, basically, it's becoming more pronounced. The teasing about her weight hasn't helped, but I've tried to put a stop to that."

"How come we're only hearing about this now?" Janice says.

Ms. Matthews looks wistfully toward the window, out to the manicured green of the hockey pitch, where girls in yellow gym gear gambol like lambs, despite a biting November wind. "I did mention it to Becky's dad," she says, "at the parent-teacher meeting." She rests her hand on the pack of coloring pencils as if it were a talisman. "I understand," she says, "that there are problems at home?"

"What do you mean?"

"Becky mentioned there are tensions. . . ."

There will most certainly be tensions, Janice thinks, when she gets home and speaks to Becky. She has an urge to find Becky's classroom and drag her outside by the scruff of the neck, to ask what she thinks she is doing, discussing their business, their private business, with this stranger. "I don't know what you're talking about," she says.

Ms. Matthews opens her mouth. This is where a little age might have saved her, where a year or two might have made all the difference, but she really is the girl Janice has taken her for, and so she says, "I meant between you and

Becky's father." Her position shifts slightly toward the door, her body ahead of her mind, readying for flight.

Janice wants to grab her by the hair and slap her. She knows what Ms. Matthews is trying to say, knows also that she must not be allowed to say it. Ms. Matthews is speaking again, the thing that she must not say twisting on her tongue, emerging in hesitant darts of words and phrases.

On the other side of the room, beneath a poster of the Gobi Desert, is a wastepaper basket. Janice makes it to the basket in time to vomit. She vomits all over an empty juice carton and pencil shavings curled like a ribbon of orange peel. Then she vomits again. She straightens up, wipes her mouth with her hand. Her eyes are wet and she dries them with her sleeve, but more wetness rises up and she realizes she is crying. Walking to the door of the classroom, she glances at Ms. Matthews and sees that she looks stricken, shocked; more shocked, Janice thinks, than if she had gone ahead and slapped her.

A foot, once bound, will be bound forever: Few can withstand the pain when bones awaken. Tend to it carefully, but always in darkness. The beauty snared beneath the bandages may dissipate in light.

SHE SITS IN A café for a few hours until the staff put the chairs on the tables and begin to mop around her feet. When eventually she goes home, she finds the hall and the downstairs rooms in darkness, save for the flicker of the TV in the living room. Becky is sprawled on the couch, her feet bound in white bandages and propped on a beanbag. Janice switches on the light. "Becky," she says. "We need to talk."

Becky blinks, rubs her eyes. She mutters something under her breath, then picks up the remote and begins surfing channels.

Janice positions herself between her daughter and the screen. "I went to see Ms. Matthews today."

Becky puts down the remote, letting the TV come to rest on a cartoon station.

"Your father and I are very happy, Becky. Do you understand that?"

Becky stares at her mutely.

"And if you ever have worries about that, or any worries at all, you come to me first, okay? I'm not blaming you for anything, Becky, please don't think I'm blaming you, but we're a family, we're a team, and we need to trust each other."

Becky is examining her fingernails, poking at her cuticles.

Janice sighs. "All right," she says. "I'm going to make a start on dinner. Then we're going to sit down together and you're going to tell me what you said to Ms. Matthews."

"I can't really remember," Becky says. "We talked about lots of stuff."

Janice feels the nausea returning. "You must try to remember," she says. "It's important." She nods at Becky's feet. "And I know that's not homework, so take off those bandages."

Becky gives no indication of having heard.

"I said take them off, Becky."

Slowly, Becky raises one foot onto the couch and begins to unwind the bandages, letting them fall in spirals to the floor. Underneath, her foot looks white and pale and startled. Red marks run across her toes where, Janice sees now, she has used elastic bands to hold the tights in place. Becky examines her toes, the arch of her foot. Her small toe is a bluish-white color, beginning to pinken as the blood comes rushing back. She forgets for a moment that she is fighting with her mother. "Look," she says, holding up her foot, "it's got smaller."

Janice bends and squints at her daughter's foot. "It's exactly the same size it always was."

"It's not," Becky says. "It's smaller." She gets up and hops across the floor to where she has left a pair of canvas pumps. She slides her bare foot into one and wriggles it around. "See?" she says, "it's loose. It wasn't loose before." She hops back across the room and flops onto the couch. She reaches for a strip of cloth from the floor.

"What are you doing?"

"I'm going to sleep in them, see what my feet are like in the morning."

"You most certainly are not."

"You hate me," Becky says. "You want me to have big, ugly clown feet like Ms. Roberts."

Janice pulls the strip of fabric from her daughter's hand, rips it in half, then in half again, and flings the pieces onto the carpet.

"Stop it! You're ruining them!" Becky jumps up, swaying a little, hopping on her one bare foot. She tries to gather the strips, but Janice kicks them, sends them scattering across the floor. "I hate you!" Becky screams. "I wish you weren't my mother. I wish I had any other mother in the world except you." She hobbles to the stairs, one foot still bandaged. Holding on to the banisters, she hops up the first set of steps, stopping to rest on the half landing.

"Get down here now," Janice says. She begins to climb the stairs after her daughter.

Becky shakes her head. Outside on the street, the lamps come on, a soft glow falling on the stairs, on the table with its crystal animals, glittering as if they'd been torched, sparking with light and fire. Becky, in that instant, is alight, too, as fierce and beautiful as a starlet from an old black-and-white movie, her hair falling loose of its bun, her face flushed. And in the next moment, she is a child again, dismayed, confused, scorched by the life sap bubbling up through her.

Janice is beside her now. "Come on, Becky, you're being silly."

Becky wipes away a tear. "Yeah?" she says. "Well, maybe I'm silly, but at least I'm not fucking pathetic. No wonder Dad hates you."

Her hand catches Becky high on the cheek, just below her left eye. She watches, as if in slow motion, her daughter toppling backward, the table crashing to the floor. The little figurines collide as they fall, cracking, splintering, slivers of crystal lodging like miniature stalagmites in the carpet. And in the immediate aftermath, just for a second, there is utter and complete silence; that brief, fleeting silence she has heard described on television by survivors of terrorist attacks and explosions. Becky gets shakily to her feet, putting one hand to the wall to steady herself. Her face is pale, apart from a red gash beneath her eye that has already started to bleed.

"Oh no," Janice whispers. "Oh no." She sinks down beside the upturned table, the floor all around glinting with shards of birds and animals. She looks at her hand, tingling still from the force of the slap. The ring on her middle finger was a gift from Philip years back that she has kept meaning to get resized. It has slid around, as it is wont to do, the stones now to the underside, a hard ridge of diamonds.

Becky puts a hand to her cut cheek. She barely seems to register the blood on her fingers when she takes them away. As if in a daze, she rights the table, returns it to its position beneath the window. Then she drops to her hands and knees and begins to gather up the crystals: the ones that have survived and the broken ones, dozens of severed limbs and shattered torsos.

"Don't," Janice says, sobbing. "Don't bother. There's no point." Reaching out, she traces a finger along the trail of blood on her daughter's face. "He will leave me now," she whispers. "He will never stay with me after this."

How beautiful the tiny slippers, the swaying walk, that will forever keep her from the fields. Let her begin now her dowry: slippers embroidered with fish and lotus flowers, crafted by her own hands.

THERE IS A CRAB apple tree, planted by a previous owner, at the end of the garden, the ground all around a pulp of bruised windfalls, though she had sworn that this year she would harvest them. She leans against the trunk, listening to the river flowing by on the other side of the fence. Looking back at the house, she sees that the light is on in Becky's bedroom, the curtains closed. Later, lights come on downstairs and she sees Philip moving about the kitchen, and she makes her way back up the garden to the house.

When she slides open the patio doors, she sees that she has startled him. He still has his coat on and is taking a beer from the fridge. He turns and she studies his face from across the kitchen, trying to gauge what he knows. "You scared me," he says. "I didn't realize you were home. Where's Becky?"

When she doesn't say anything, he comes over and puts an arm around her shoulder. "You're not still mad at me, are you?" he says. "I thought we were okay," and he kisses her on the forehead.

"Philip . . ." she begins, but overhead a door opens, and she hears footsteps coming down the stairs. She moves away from her husband, goes to stand at the far side of the room.

Becky's hair hangs down her back in a single plait, and she no longer looks fourteen but like a child of eleven or twelve. She has washed her face and put a Band-Aid on her cheek, a square fabric dressing that covers not just the cut but the skin all around, too. She has removed all the bandages and her feet are in a pair of pink slippers.

"Hey, princess," Philip says. "What happened to your face?" He puts down his beer and goes over to her. "Did something happen at school? If something's happening at school you need to tell us. Janice, have you seen this?"

Becky winces as he touches her cheek. "I fell against the fence playing hockey," she says. "It's only a scratch."

"Let me see," he says, but she takes a step back.

"It's fine, honestly," she says, "Mum had a look already. She put some antiseptic on it."

He throws his hands up in a gesture of defeat. "Okay," he says. "I guess you girls have it under control." Picking up his beer, he goes out to the living room.

Later, while Philip is watching TV, Janice goes quietly upstairs. On the half landing, she sees the crystal animals have been reassembled, the casualties glued back together, crudely but effectively, each figure back in its correct place. She stops outside Becky's bedroom and listens. There is no noise, apart from a soft, papery sound, like pages turning. She tries the door handle but it is locked, and then even the paper sounds stop, and it is so quiet she can hear Mrs. Harding through the walls, moving around the house next door.

She considers calling to Becky through the door, but doesn't know what to say, and is afraid Philip might hear. After a few minutes, she goes back downstairs.

It has started to rain, a drizzle first that quickly becomes a slanting downpour, hammering against the glass of the patio doors. She sits at the kitchen table, looking out at the darkness of the garden, watching rainwater leak through the center join of the doors to form a puddle on the kitchen floor. She watches the puddle grow larger, not bothering, as she would usually do, to fetch a mop and bucket. It is something that happens every time it rains, a fault dating to the doors' original installation. She has meant to get them fixed, or replaced, but it will be impossible to find a tradesperson this close to Christmas. She will wait until January, when things are quieter. She will do it then.

> *A man will seldom touch a bound foot. Knowing this, into the smallest of her slippers, let her sew a pouch: There she will keep her darkest secrets.*

THOSE THAT I FIGHT
I DO NOT HATE

———

Ranelagh on a summer Saturday, the pavements scattered with blossoms, the air pulsating with the rhythmic thrum of lawnmowers. Kevin stood at the window of the Millers' living room, watching a dozen or so little girls pose for photos in the front garden. His own daughter was among them, her blond curls straightened and pinned in a plait, so that at first, in the midst of so many other plaited heads, he hardly recognized her. The Millers lived in a red-brick Victorian near the church, and Fiona Miller had insisted on the party. It was no trouble, she told anyone who attempted to cry off. It would be a treat for the children, and she and Bob were happy to host it, knowing as they did that not everyone was as fortunate as themselves. The girls shrieked and giggled, buzzing with sugar and summer, and then, remembering themselves, they smoothed the skirts of their white dresses and raised small, careful hands to adjust veils and tiaras. "Lovely, aren't they?" Kevin said, turning to the woman behind the drinks table. The woman frowned. She wasn't the caterer but one of Fiona Miller's friends, perhaps even one of her sisters, and this placed her firmly in the ranks of people who hated him. "Great that the rain's held off," he said, because she could hardly find that objectionable, but she began to move bottles around the table as if they were chess pieces, taking them by the necks, setting them down in their new positions with unmistakable hostility.

Sun angled through the slatted blinds, igniting the glitter of cards on the mantelpiece, bouncing off the guns of Bob Miller's favorite model plane—a WWI Sopwith Camel—displayed on a stand beside the door. Bob's great-grandfather had served in the London Irish Rifles, losing an arm at Flers-Courcelette. His uniform, and his cap with its badge of harp and crown, was displayed in a large glass case at the end of the Millers' hall. Also in the case were things belonging to other dead men: bullets, armbands, and letters that Bob had purchased on the Internet. Bob liked to joke that he'd been a military man in a previous life, though in this one he was senior actuary for an insurance company. Kevin turned again to the window. His wife was in the garden also, talking, he saw now, to the man who'd once been his boss. Earlier, he and the man had exchanged terse hellos in the hallway. He'd asked Kevin—and why did everyone feel obliged to ask?—if anything had turned up yet, and with that out of the way, had retreated to a suitable distance. Kevin watched the man rest a hand consolingly on his wife's arm, while she dabbed at her eyes with a hankie. He needed a drink. He'd hoped the woman at the table might have gone to join the others in the garden, but she remained at her post, arms folded across her chest. On his way out of the room, he touched a finger to the propellers of the little plane, sending the blades spinning into a blur of wood and metal.

He'd brought a flask of vodka for this eventuality, stashed in the inside pocket of his jacket. But he'd been relieved of the jacket as soon as he arrived by Aoife, the Millers' older daughter. "It's okay," he'd said. "I'll hold on to it. It's a bit chilly"—though it was late May, the day warm, the air thick with pollen and silky parachutes of dandelion seed that blew in white gusts down the avenue. Aoife—outraged at being on cloakroom duty—had manhandled the jacket off him anyway, and now he felt the missing flask like a phantom limb. As he walked toward the kitchen, the front door opened and the small girls came hurtling down the hall, one of them with a parasol tucked under her arm like a bayonet. He flattened himself against the wall as they went by, a battalion of miniature brides, their white sandals clattering over the tiles. A veil brushed against his arm, the scratch of gauze surprisingly rough. At the end of the Millers' hall, before the glass case with the disembodied uniform, the girls veered left into the music room, and from there out to the garden to race in circles around the house, their cries rising and falling in Doppler effect.

Fiona Miller was in the kitchen squeezing oranges. She was a dark-haired, tanned woman a few years his senior. "You shouldn't have come," she said. She was using an electric juicer, feeding plump oranges in at one end, harvesting slow dribbles in a jug at the other.

"You invited me."

"I had to invite you. But you shouldn't have come. What were you thinking, Kevin?"

She had always made him feel small; small and red-necked and lacking in etiquette. What about all that fucking we did? he wanted to say. Where was the etiquette in that? Instead he said, "Does Bob know?" Knowing very well that Bob didn't.

"Don't do this to me, Kevin," she said. "Because if you do, I'm warning you, you'll be sorry." She picked up two more oranges and flung them into the juicer. She was wearing a low-cut black dress, and he couldn't help thinking that her breasts were like two small oranges, and that the nipples pressing against the fabric were like little hard pips. He remembered how they used to feel in his hands, and when his eyes moved back to her face, he saw that she was watching him watching her, and he looked away, out to the hall where his wife was talking to one of the other mothers. She was holding several parasols, none of which belonged to their own daughter; his mother-in-law, who had paid for the outfit, thought parasols tacky. His wife glanced in his direction. It was one of the advantages of being with someone a very long time that he could tell instantly, even at a distance, that she was angry.

The juicer sputtered to a stop. "I'm out of oranges," Fiona said.

"I'll get some," he said, sensing an opportunity, because there was a liquor store in the village.

"Aoife will get them. She can go on her bike. It won't take her a minute." Fiona banged on the kitchen window. Aoife was sitting on a swing in the back garden, talking on her phone. She looked up and pulled a face at her mother, but didn't budge. Her mother banged on the glass again. Aoife slid slowly, insolently, off the swing and began to walk toward the house.

"How old is she now?" he said. "Sixteen?"

"Eighteen next month. Which means we'll have to do this whole bloody thing all over again."

"Well, I won't come," he said. "So you needn't worry."

"I'm not worried," she said. "You're not invited."

Aoife arrived in from the garden, slamming the back door behind her. She snatched the ten-euro note her mother handed her. "Oranges," Fiona said. "Two nets, and make sure they're properly ripe." Aoife rolled her eyes and left.

There came the sound of feet plodding down the hall, and a wet, wheezy sigh. Bob Miller was unlikely to take anyone by stealth. "Beer, Kev?" he said, opening the fridge, and then, before Kevin could answer, "I mean, Coke?"

"No, thanks."

Bob cracked open a can for himself. "Long time no see," he said. "I was only saying to Fiona this morning: When was the last time we saw Kevin, and we couldn't remember, could we, Fiona?"

Fiona was slapping a wet cloth—randomly, it seemed to Kevin—over kitchen surfaces. Now she went to squeeze the cloth out in the sink, at the same time running fresh water noisily into a basin.

"So," Bob said, "what've you been getting up to?"

"Nothing much."

"Anything turn up yet?"

"Not yet."

"Have you tried JobBridge?"

A small, weeping child with a grazed knee came into the kitchen. She was followed by four other children who formed a circle as Fiona applied ointment—none too gently, Kevin noticed—and a Band-Aid. No sooner had the children been dispatched outside than Aoife returned, her cheeks flushed from the bicycle, wisps of dandelion seed caught in her hair. She flung a plastic bag onto the kitchen island. "These are mandarins," Fiona said, peering into the bag, but Aoife had already flounced out to the garden to resume her position on the swing. Bob winked. "The joys, eh, Kev?" he said, and he flopped into a chair in the corner. Fiona took the oranges, or mandarins, to the sink and began to scrub them with a wire brush as if they'd been rolling around the floor of a nuclear waste facility. She piled them into a bowl before proceeding to drop them one by one into the juicer, and the slow dribble started up again.

"Excuse me," Kevin said, pretending to check his phone. "I need to take a call." Once in the hall, he went to the door of the living room and looked in. The woman at the drinks table still hadn't moved from her station. She was busy now; the caterers had set out trays of salads and cold meats, and everybody had come in from the garden. He considered where Aoife might have put his jacket. He'd been in this house many times, mostly times when he shouldn't have been.

On the half landing, he paused to inspect the photographs. He didn't recall noticing them before, but then before, his mind would have been on the curve of Fiona's hips as she climbed the stairs ahead of him. They weren't the usual snaps of seasides or birthdays, but black-and-white photographs of war. Biplanes rose from scorched airstrips, into skies black and hellish with smoke. Hollow-eyed soldiers in steel Brodie helmets lay on their stomachs in the mud. How he envied Bob Miller. He didn't envy him the photographs—ghoulish things that already had triggered the early stirrings of nausea. Nor did he envy him his wife, his house, or his job, though there'd been a time when he'd envied all of these things. No, what he envied most was Bob Miller's want of imagination, a want that saved even as it failed, that allowed Bob to make a hobby of war, to gaze with complacency upon the horror of others, happy it hadn't come for him, certain it never would. Lucky, lucky Bob who knew so little pain that he must order it neatly packaged on eBay, to hang in lacquered frames on his wall.

In the spare room, the coats lay on the bed in a tangle of empty sleeves. Several had slid from the heap onto the carpet. He went through the ones on the bed first, lifting them, setting them aside until, halfway through, he found his jacket. When he picked it up, its lightness registered with him on some subterranean, animal level before the thought had even formed in his brain. The flask was missing. He searched beneath the remainder of the coats on the bed, then started on the pile on the floor.

"All right, Kev?"

He was holding a woman's green blazer in his hands when he turned to see Bob in the doorway. "Grand, Bob," he said. "I was just looking for my car keys."

"You're not thinking of driving, Kev?"

"I need to get something from the car." He floundered about, mentally, for something plausible. "An inhaler. For my daughter."

"Well, then," Bob said, "we'd better find those keys," and he bent to lift a man's navy overcoat from the floor.

Kevin had a sudden vision of Bob finding the flask. "Thanks, Bob," he said, "but I've already found them, actually." He patted the pocket of his jeans. "They were under the valance."

Bob straightened up. He looked confused. "Right," he said.

Kevin realized he was still holding the blazer, and tossed it quickly onto the bed. They stood in awkward silence for a moment, staring at each other, while through the open window came the shrill laughter of small girls playing tag on the Millers' driveway.

"I guess we can go back downstairs," Bob said.

"Okay, then."

"Okay."

Bob gestured for Kevin to exit the room ahead of him, and when they were both outside, he pulled the door shut and took something from his pocket. There followed the excruciating sound of the key turning in the lock. The men descended the stairs together, careful not to make eye contact, neither of them speaking. When they reached the bottom, Kevin didn't stop but kept on walking, down the hall and out the front door, across the cobble-lock drive to the pavement where his wife had parked their car by the curb. He leaned against the garden wall and stared at the car. He didn't have the keys; his wife had them. These days, she was careful to keep them on her person at all times. He had a sense of somebody watching him, and knew that if he turned it would be Bob, but he didn't turn. Let him watch, he thought, because here on the street it was peaceful, the air clean and sweet smelling, the only noise the yapping of a small dog farther along the avenue. In the distance, beyond the village, beyond the city, he saw fields and hills, green unpeopled expanses not yet spoiled.

When he went back inside, a cake was being cut in the

sunroom, a giant three-tiered confection topped with a troupe of miniature white-iced girls in white-iced dresses. The real girls were seated around a trestle table, protective plastic covers over their clothes. His wife was at one end of the table, passing around slices of cake and plastic cutlery, but he didn't go in. Instead, he went to the living room where, with a heady feeling approaching joy, he found the drinks table deserted. It was a wasteland of empty bottles, wine, Pimm's, prosecco, but in the middle of the debris was a bottle of vodka, practically untouched.

In the kitchen, he poured orange juice into a glass. Through the window he saw Aoife on the swing, her long legs dangling, the toes of her white Converses scuffing the dust. She was nothing like her father; Bob's genes had lost that particular skirmish. Instead, she was slim and dark and pretty, how he imagined Fiona must have been at that age. He watched her for a moment, then poured a second glass of juice and went out to the garden, taking the vodka and the glasses with him. The expression on her face bordered on a sneer, but she brightened when she saw the bottle. The day had remained fine, but there was something ominous in the stillness of the clouds, as if now that they had stopped moving, they might suddenly drop to earth. Aoife hopped off the swing. "This way," she said, indicating a gap in the hedge. "They don't like it when I drink."

"They don't like it when I drink, either," he said.

When she laughed it was her mother's laugh, uncouth with a hint of scorn, and her legs, when she settled herself beside him in the grass behind the hedge, were her mother's legs, long and tanned and small boned. She giggled as he poured the vodka, and when she turned to smile at him, he noticed her eyes were slightly glazed. They were sitting in a wilderness of long grass and weeds, a narrow strip of no-man's-land between the backs of the houses and a walled public green. Dog daisies and poppies grew wild and riot-ous, spilling petals and seeds onto the ground. He felt the jut of her hip as she edged closer to him, and as her long hair brushed against his arm, he caught a scent of vanilla and something else, something young and girlish, like apples or berries. He drank some vodka and looked up at the sky. The clouds seemed grayer and darker and were no longer still, but moved erratically, bulging against their casing of sky. It was as if something behind them was trying to break through, pushing them forward in a thick, billowing mass, so that they blew not like clouds, but smoke. As he watched, he saw in their depths quick and sudden flashes of silver. It might have been a final rallying of sun, but it reminded him of the light glinting on the metal guns of Bob Miller's model Sopwith Camel. And as he touched a hand to her cheek, he knew the sound he heard in the distance was not the hum of lawnmowers, but the drone of low-flying aircraft.

ALL ABOUT ALICE

———

AUGUST WAS HEAVY WITH DYING BLUEBOTTLES. THEY gathered in velvety blue droves on the windowpanes and beat their gauzy wings against the glass. They squatted black and languid along the sills. Alice slouched low in an armchair in the kitchen, watching her father's curious ballet. The bottoms of his trousers, rolled high above his ankles, unfurled a little further with every stumbling jeté. His newspaper carved frantic circles in the air as he struck at the flies.

"Feckers," he shouted. "Hoors."

Maddened, the bluebottles looped like Spitfires. They ricocheted off the lampshades and pinged off the cabinets that held Alice's Irish dancing medals. One came to rest, dark and glittering, on the television. *Thwack!* and a fly dropped to the floor. Alice stared out the window as the kitchen rang with the crunch of bluebottle on linoleum.

Outside in the yard, Sunday had stilled the galvanized roof of the bathroom extension, taking away the rattle of passing lorries and leaving instead a dusting of early leaves that settled along the ridges. A stray plastic bag fluttered in the bushes inside the gate. Alice's father flopped into his chair, flushed and triumphant. He brushed a translucent wing from the front of the sports section and turned the page.

"More tea, Daddy?" Alice made no attempt to reach for the teapot. Her father never had more tea. On the table beside him, his pills were lined up in dazzling technicolor. Alice glanced at the clock. Half past ten. At four o'clock her father would catch a bus to West Cork to holiday for a week with his cousin, Olive. His suitcase had been standing in the hall for the past three days. Alice, too, had been marking time, counting the days, giddy at the prospect of having the house to herself. She was forty-five.

ON MONDAY MORNING, IN her first act of delinquency since her father's departure, Alice hung flypaper from the ceiling. Her father hated flypaper. Soon there was a dead bluebottle twisting overhead as Alice drank her tea. After breakfast, she took the dishes to the sink, leaving them to soak in a pan of scummy water. On a shelf above the sink was a photograph of a reproachful-looking woman in her mid- to late sixties, hair pulled back in a tightly wound bun. Her eyes, like Alice's eyes, were gray flecked with green. A man had once told Alice that her eyes were the color of a storm at sea, but the eyes that stared out from the photograph were sunken and passive. Poor Mammy.

Alice took a mug of tea out to the good sitting room. She examined her reflection in the mirror. Her time away had brought lines and shadows that deepened with every passing year. She sat on the sofa, its floral print faded from dust and sunlight, and thought about what she might do. A whole week stretched in front of her: a Wild West of freedom, waiting for the charge of Alice's wagon. There came to her then a memory, a fragment of a morning from many years ago: Barcelona with sun angling through a chink of white curtain, the crumbs of yellow madeleines scattered across her plate at breakfast. And afterward the city, vast and glorious, shimmering in front of her.

Alice felt hope stir in her stomach, felt it slosh gently with the tea. She wanted to leave her life like a balloon leaves a fairground. To slip from life's sweaty hand and float away. She looked at her watch. She thought of her father walking the beach with Olive, stepping on bubbles of black seaweed, hearing them pop. Time was ticking. She went over to the window, looked out at the straggle of gray buildings along Main Street, and wondered again what she should do with the day until at last it came to her. She would make a batch of queen cakes and take them down to Marian's.

"IT'S NOT ALL ROMANCE, you know, Alice. You're thinking, there's Marian with her perfect house and her perfect husband and a brand-new Fiesta outside the door. Well, I'll be straight with you, Alice, since you've asked: It's not all moonlight and roses."

Alice was fairly sure she hadn't asked. Marian had answered the door with the new baby over her shoulder and the toddler around her ankles. Now she was moving in a slow waltz over the kitchen tiles, a tea towel under her foot, mopping up baby-sick. With every turn, the baby dripped more vomit over her shoulder.

Through the patio doors to the garden, Alice could see sunlight dancing off the silver cover of the barbecue and warming the varnished oak decking. It highlighted the tasteful creams and taupes of the patio furniture and lingered among the late-summer flowers that bloomed in terra-cotta pots. Since Marian had married Eugene it was all "barbecues" and "suppers" and stainless steel patio heaters. Alice smoothed down her new sequined top and waited for Marian to admire it. But today Marian was missing her cues, fluffing her lines. She was more preoccupied than usual with the dribbled demands of the children.

"Issy good boy? Issy? Yessy issy!" Marian was hunched over the baby on the sofa, changing his nappy. "Toe-toes, toe-toes," she said, putting the baby's pink, dimpled foot to her lips, pretending to eat it. The baby wriggled in delight, gurgled, and Marian nibbled at his toes and laughed back at him. Alice boiled the kettle and searched the cupboard for a clean plate for the queen cakes. She began to arrange them in neat circles.

"Where do you keep the tea bags?"

Marian took the baby's foot out of her mouth and looked around, disoriented. It was as if she had forgotten all about Alice. "Eugene won't have them in the house," she said. "Carcinogenic."

"Tea bags?"

"Yes, even the organic ones. Would you believe it?"

Marian put the baby wriggling on his back in the play-pen, then scooped the toddler off the floor and set him down next to the baby. She made a pot of loose-leaf tea and sat down opposite Alice.

"Thanks for the muffins." It was always "muffins" with Marian these days. Marian never said "queen cakes" any-more, now that she was married to Eugene.

"Daddy's away this week," Alice said.

"I heard."

"I thought I might as well do something."

Marian picked up a carton of milk, splashed some in her tea. "Like what?"

Alice shrugged. "I don't know. Meet someone."

Marian sighed, mopped up cake crumbs with her finger, popped them in her mouth. "You mean a man?"

Alice nodded.

"The trouble with the men around here, Alice, is that they all know you."

"I thought I might go up to Dublin," Alice said.

Marian shook her head. "Too dangerous."

"Speed dating?"

"Too many time wasters."

Alice felt the morning's hope begin to curdle in her stomach. She tried again. "I could go to a nightclub."

"On your own?" Marian was talking with her mouth full. "There's a lot expected of a girl nowadays." She gave Alice a meaningful look. "Stuff you've never even heard of."

Marian, Alice thought, was talking as if she were the only one in this town who ever had sex. Talking as if she knew all about Alice. Alice wanted to tell Marian that last night she had made love out in the back of the town hall to a sound engineer from somewhere foreign, tattoos all over his body. She hadn't, of course. Last night Alice had fallen asleep in an armchair and had woken cold and cramped in the small hours, a mug of stale tea on the table beside her. The truth was that Alice had not slept with a man in four years. And Marian, like everybody else in this town, really did know all about Alice.

Alice had reached the bottom of her teacup. She was afraid to look in case a pattern might form among the leaves. She was afraid she might have the gift. Poor Mammy had the gift and much good it did her. Instead, she looked across the table at Marian, at the dark circles beneath her eyes, the greasy hair, the baby-sick on her cardigan. She saw with sudden clarity the desolate wasteland of her friend's ruin and, just as clearly, saw it mirror her own. She felt the sun wane, felt the evening and the kitchen closing in.

A whole day had slipped away from her. "Does Eugene have any friends?" Alice felt a fragment of queen cake lodge in her throat at the mention of Eugene, that beige, insipid man. The children were wailing now and Marian was back at the playpen, a grizzling baby over her shoulder. The toddler began to choke, and Marian stooped to take a plastic cow from its mouth. When she straightened up again she said: "There's a couple of new guys on the soccer team. They're coming over tomorrow evening for a barbecue. You could drop by, see what happens."

She sat down opposite Alice again with the baby on her knee. She stood the plastic cow, still glistening with spit, on the table between them. "These are young lads up from Limerick," she said. Her eyes left the soft fuzz of the baby's head for a moment and fixed on Alice. "They don't know anyone around here." She looked away then, out through the patio doors to the garden where a breeze was buffeting the flowers in the terra-cotta pots. "All I'm saying," she said, "is play your cards right. There's no need to go telling them your age. No need to go telling them anything."

NOT COUNTING THE BABIES, there were six people at Marian's barbecue. Marian and Eugene were on the deck, arguing over raw sausages. One of the lads from the soccer team had brought his girlfriend, a whippet-thin girl of about eighteen with a piercing in her lip. Alice sat at the patio table with a man called Jarlath, watching a wasp drown in a jam jar. Jarlath was in his late twenties, thirty at most. His hair was beginning an early retreat from his temples. He had no baggage, at least none that Alice had been able to establish. It was unlikely, as Poor Mammy might have said, that there had been any great rush on him. He was not the best-looking man in the world, nor the most eloquent. Still, he was broad shouldered and tall and Alice liked the way he blushed when he spoke to her.

"So," Jarlath said. "Marian told me you used to be an Irish dancing teacher."

Marian, Alice thought, had no sense. It might seem harmless enough, but Alice knew from experience that it was just a short hop, just a skitter of vowels and consonants, to why she was no longer a dancing teacher. Alice knew there was no bolt to slide across her past. The past was an open door and the best that could be done was to hurry by on the corridor. She sighed and dragged her chair closer to Jarlath's so that their thighs brushed. "Enough about me," she said.

Earlier that afternoon, Alice's father had telephoned from West Cork to remind Alice to put the trash out and to sign for her dole, even though Alice had been unemployed for years now. At the end of the evening, Jarlath didn't ask for her phone number, but Alice wrote it on a paper napkin and gave it to him anyway.

For the next two days, Alice sat in the kitchen, drank tea, and waited. Corpses of flies multiplied on the flypaper. She got a cloth and dusted her mother's photograph. Poor Mammy. She had gone downhill very quickly while Alice was away; everyone had said so. Alice had come back to a straw woman. Pneumonia, it had said on the death cert. It might just as well have said "Alice."

On Thursday afternoon, the phone rang. It was Alice's father telling her to order a piece of back bacon from the butcher for Sunday, nothing too big and not too much fat. There was still no word from Jarlath. On Thursday evening, Alice put on blusher, lipstick, and her lowest cut sequined top and waited outside the soccer grounds. When Jarlath saw her he froze. For an excruciating moment it looked like he might keep walking, but instead he came over and stood silently in front of her, and Alice did the rest.

IN THE SEMIDARKNESS OF Jarlath's bedroom, Alice lay on her back. She saw a large amoeba-shaped stain on the ceiling, and, on top of the wardrobe, an orange traffic cone. Downstairs, the two young men that Jarlath shared the house with had turned the music up louder. Jarlath lay next to her, his jeans still around his ankles. The music stopped downstairs and for a while there was silence except for the sound of a car going by on the street outside. Alice was overcome by a deadly urge to talk.

"I was away for a while."

Jarlath's fingers paused in their downward descent along her body and rose to wait in a holding pattern above her navel. "Holidays?"

Alice rolled onto her side to face him. "Jarlath," she said, "have you ever done something you've really regretted?"

Jarlath shrugged and said nothing.

"Once," Alice said, "when I was still a dancing teacher, I fell in love with the father of one of my pupils. He lived in one of those big houses across the river. His wife lives there still."

The muffled sounds of late summer filtered through the curtains: the high-pitched barking of small dogs, the buzz of weed trimmers, the shrill mating calls of teenagers.

"I thought it was love," Alice said. She laughed, but the laugh bounced off the walls of the bedroom and boomeranged back at her. "He took me to Barcelona once for a weekend." She raised herself up on one elbow. "Have you ever been to Barcelona?"

Jarlath shook his head. He had moved almost imperceptibly away from her in the bed and had started to pull up his trousers.

"You should see it," Alice said. "It's beautiful." She watched Jarlath struggling into his jeans, fumbling with the zipper. Earlier, during sex, she had surprised him with her vigor. Marian would have been impressed. "When he tried to end it," Alice said, "I panicked. I told him I would tell his wife."

It was getting late, the room edging closer to darkness. Jarlath sat on the bed, lacing up his boots. Every word that bubbled up onto Alice's tongue seemed to swallow a little more of what light remained, but she could not help herself.

"Of course I would never have told his wife." Her eyes followed Jarlath as he bent to pick his shirt up from the floor.

"But he believed I would. He gave me ten grand to keep quiet."

Jarlath stopped buttoning his shirt. "Ten grand?"

Alice nodded. "I took my mother to London to visit her brother, I changed the car, and I bought new linoleum for the kitchen. Then I asked him for more."

"Did he pay?"

"He kept paying for two years, and then he went to the police."

Jarlath was standing by the foot of the bed. Behind him on the wall was a ragged-edged poster of Radiohead, defaced with graffiti. Alice noticed how here in his bedroom, with his face flushed and his hair damp with sweat, he seemed much younger than he had at the barbecue.

"So what happened?"

"I went to jail," Alice said. "It was all over the newspapers. Poor Mammy took it very badly; Poor Mammy thought I was still a virgin."

Jarlath shuffled his feet on the carpet and looked away. Alice felt sorry for him.

"He left his wife anyway," she said. "That first summer I was away, he disappeared with a Portuguese woman who came to work in the hotel."

"Where did they go?"

Alice shrugged. "Someplace far away."

Jarlath came round to the side of the bed and stooped to give her a hug. It was a safe, compassionate hug, the kind of hug her cousin, Olive, might give Alice's father when she put him on the bus home Sunday morning. He touched her bare shoulder. "Take care of yourself," he said.

Alice watched Jarlath putting on his jacket, getting ready to leave his own house. She knew that she had said too much, knew that Marian would roll her eyes and be furious, but there was no stopping now. She sat up in bed, clutching the sheets to her breasts. "I'm forty-five," she said.

HER FATHER'S SUITCASE IS back in the hall, waiting to be unpacked and stored beneath the stairs for another year, or maybe another couple of years. Alice has taken down all the flypaper. "Tea, Daddy?" She pours a cup of tea for her father, sets it down in his saucer with a fistful of colored pills. But her father is on his feet, prowling the kitchen with a rolled-up newspaper. "Hoors," he shouts. "Feckers." There is a stirring in the folds of the curtains, a murmur in the clammy air of the kitchen. And all along the windowpanes, the bluebottles, dark and velvety, rise up in a last frantic salute to life and summer. And they buzz and ping and beat their gauzy wings against the glass.

ALONG THE
HERON-STUDDED RIVER

———

HE GRIPPED THE ICE SCRAPER IN HIS GLOVED HANDS,
pulled it back and forth across the windscreen. A mist of ice
particles rose up, settled upon the car bonnet. It was dark
yet, but the sun was beginning to rise, tingeing the white
fields pink. All around him the land was hard and still, the
ditch that separated their property from the farm next door
brittle grassed and silver. In the distance he could see the
line of trees that flanked the river, their branches dusted with
a light powdering of snow. A heron stood beside the small
ornamental pond, stabbing the frozen surface with its beak.
The previous Saturday, Cathy had driven to the city and had
returned with half a dozen koi, some of them bronze and
tea colored, others gray. He had watched her release them,

dazed and startled, into the pond. Dropping the ice scraper, he clapped his hands and the heron rose up and flew away.

The house was a dormer bungalow, facing south toward the river, set into a hollow in the field. From where he stood in the driveway, it looked like a Christmas ornament, frost clinging to the roof, condensation rounding the squares of light in the windows. He could see Cathy moving about the kitchen in her dressing gown, Gracie on her hip, preparing breakfast.

"Did you get any sleep?" he had asked earlier.

"Yes," she said, "plenty," but he had felt her slip from their bed during the night, had heard her feet on the floorboards as she went downstairs. He knew she would be on the phone to Martha, her sister, who lived in Castleisland. What Martha made of these late-night phone calls, he didn't know. Martha spoke to him only when matters concerning Cathy or Gracie required it, grudgingly even then, and once a month she posted a check for the daycare fees.

He finished the windscreen, leaving the engine running so the car might heat up, and went back into the house. In the hall he removed his wet gloves and put them to dry on the radiator. He could hear his wife and daughter in the kitchen singing "Incy Wincy Spider." He watched them through the door, their forms distorted by the patterned glass. Cathy was making porridge. She balanced the wooden spoon on the edge of the pot and shimmied low to the floor, her dressing gown enfolding Gracie like a tent. Gracie screamed and wriggled out, then immediately crawled back in again, pulling the dressing gown tight about her. She poked her face through a gap between buttons and giggled. And as he entered the room, he felt something seep away, like the slow hiss of air from a puncture.

Cathy stepped over her daughter and crossed the kitchen to kiss him on the cheek. There were dark circles under her eyes. She took both his hands in hers and rubbed them gently, frowning at their coldness.

"Is it bad?" she said, inclining her head toward the window.

"Bad enough. You'll need to be careful going to daycare later."

"It'll have thawed by then. Do you want coffee?"

He shook his head. "I'll get some at the office."

Gracie toddled across the kitchen to reclaim her mother. Cathy scooped her up and she clung, limpet-like, to her neck. Over on the burner, the porridge spluttered in its pot. "I'll do that," he said, as he saw Cathy turn. "You sit down."

He poured porridge into two bowls and carried them to the table. Cathy lowered Gracie, kicking and protesting, into her high chair and fastened the straps. "Martha's asked us to go stay with her for a few days," she said.

He pulled out a chair beside her. "When?"

"She thought next week might be good. There's a festival on, and a few of the cousins will be around." She stirred some milk into the porridge, and blew gently on a spoonful before putting it to Gracie's lips. He watched the child clamp her mouth shut, contort her small body so she was facing the other direction.

"I don't know," he said. "I worry about you being there on your own."

"We won't be on our own. We'll be with Martha." She took Gracie's chin in her hand and gently turned it back toward the spoon. "You could come down on the weekend, stay for a few days."

"Did Martha say that?" He knew how Martha felt about him. It was the same way he felt about Martha.

"You know she's always asking us to visit."

You, he thought. She's always asking you to visit, but just then Gracie released a mouthful of porridge she had quarantined in her cheek. He watched Cathy's hand dart out and catch it on the spoon. Her own porridge was untouched, solidifying into a cold gray disc.

"Here," he said, reaching for the spoon. "Let me feed her. You eat your breakfast." But she shook her head.

"I can manage," she said. "Anyway, you need to get to work."

He got up from his chair and went over to the window. Outside, light was spreading from the east. The garden was spiky with the stalks of leafless plants, and a mound of fermented lawn cuttings leaned, white-capped, against the fence. Gracie's tricycle, left out overnight, was frosted, too, snatches of purple breaking through here and there.

It was on a morning like this, white with a hush upon the

fields, that they had found the site. They had traveled from Dublin the evening before, the only accommodation a B&B in a village ten miles away where he had made cautious love to Cathy beneath thin sheets and wiry blankets. She was in the early stages of pregnancy and he had moved inside her with a new restraint, terrified that he might harm the baby, not understanding how very safe his daughter was then, how very protected. The next morning, they met the auctioneer at the field, the farmland all around them in folds of white hills like a bridal gown, jeweled with frost. Small dark birds, feathers puffed against the cold, darted in and out of hedgerows.

"Have you ever seen anything so beautiful?" Cathy had whispered. "It's like Narnia."

"Do you think you could live here?" he remembered asking, as they walked behind the auctioneer to where their car was parked in the lane. "Yes," she had answered. "Yes, I think I could."

HE LOOKED AT HIS watch and saw that it was almost eight. He went over to kiss Cathy, and as she lifted her face to his, porridge slid from the spoon and dropped onto the tray of the high chair. Gracie studied it, poked it, traced spirals with her fingers round and round the tray. Cathy just shrugged and mopped up the porridge with the sleeve of her dressing gown. There were mornings when he was unsettled by her eagerness to please him, by the transparency of her efforts to affect happiness. This morning she seemed more relaxed, brighter, her smile as she said goodbye less forced.

But a few minutes later as he sat in his car, key in the ignition, she appeared at the front door. She picked her way across the graveled driveway in thin fabric slippers, arms wrapped around herself to fend off the cold.

"You don't have to go to Manchester this month, do you?" she said, as he rolled down the window.

"No," he said. "I don't think so," and he saw relief in her face as she waved him off.

He drove out through the gate and down the lane, shattering membranes of ice stretched across the puddles, and turned onto the main road. At Twomey's bridge, a buckled fender and side panel lay bone white in the verge, like skeletons along an ancient silk route, a warning to other travelers. His phone sat on the dash. He liked to keep it where he could see it, though he knew it would not ring. Once he joined the river road he was out of coverage until he reached the dual carriageway. The river road was a portal between worlds: his home on one side, the city on the other, and in the middle a no-man's-land of space and time when his wife and daughter were beyond his grasp, unreachable.

Mist rose from the river, ghosted through black and empty trees. The herons that lived along the bank were out in force, balanced on spindly legs. They stood motionless, their long, curved necks thrust forward, as if they, too, like the trees and the grass, had been stilled by the frost. The road was rough and uneven. Every spring, the county council sent out men and machines with truckloads of asphalt to lay a new surface. And every winter the river tore it away again, so that, come February, what remained was not so much a road but a dirt track.

His office was in a 1970s square-fronted building in the city center. Steps, pockmarked with gum and doused in bleach, led to a foyer hung with advertisements for various financial products. He saw Cahill, his manager, waiting in the lift lobby and decided to take the stairs. Cahill, he knew, was losing patience. He had considered talking to Cahill, but the time had never seemed right, and now he thought the time might have passed. Lately he had noticed a change in the way Cahill spoke to him, and if they passed each other in the corridors or in the canteen, Cahill mostly looked away.

His cubicle was on the fourth floor, in a long, rectangular room with floor-to-ceiling glass windows. More glass separated the office space from the stairwell and the staff canteen. He switched on his computer and saw Cahill had included him on an email about the trip to Manchester, scheduled for the following week. He clicked "Reply," typed a couple of sentences, and stopped. For a while, he stared at the screen without typing anything, then saved the reply to "Drafts" to finish later.

He made a mug of coffee in the canteen and brought it back to his desk. The woman in the next cubicle raised her head above the partition. "Cahill was looking for you," she said, in the singsong, lisping voice that grated on him, and then she went back to work, synthetic nails scuttling click-click across her keyboard. He opened his emails and resumed the reply to Cahill. He read over what he had written, added a word or two, then closed it and started on something else.

At 11:35 A.M. his mobile rang. It was Martha. "I'm worried," she said.

He had told Martha time and again that he worked in an open-plan office.

"Hold on," he said. He got up and went out to the lobby. He pictured Martha on the other end of the phone, her cheeks sucked hollow in annoyance at being kept waiting, tugging at the buttons of her cardigan as if even they had offended her. Between the lifts and the cleaning-supplies cupboard was a narrow recessed space. He had discovered that if he pressed close against the wall, he could see his cubicle through the glass, but could not easily be seen himself.

"Okay," he said. "Go ahead."

"Have you noticed anything lately?"

"Nothing worth talking about."

"That means you've noticed something."

He wondered how two people who both loved Cathy could dislike each other so very much. "She doesn't go jogging anymore," he said, "but that's mostly down to the weather."

"Anything else?"

He imagined Martha's fidgeting becoming fiercer, a button popping off her cardigan, rolling across her kitchen floor. He closed his eyes and took a deep breath. He was about to betray his wife. "She's skipped her meds a couple of times, but only a couple. And she's tired, but then Gracie's been a handful lately."

There was silence for a moment and then Martha said, "Gracie isn't at daycare today."

"How do you know?"

"I rang the daycare and they told me."

"You had no business ringing them."

"I ring all the time," Martha said. "Somebody has to. Did you know she forgot to collect Gracie twice last week? They had to phone her when she didn't show."

"She was probably just late," he said. "Late isn't forgetting."

"She was over an hour late. And yesterday? When they were changing Gracie? Her dress was filthy. Filthy and frayed along one side, and she wasn't even wearing a vest."

He rested his forehead against the wood of the supplies cupboard, inhaled its smells of bleach and disinfectant. Every small thing had been taken from his wife's possession, laid bare under a harsh and artificial light; every failing paraded before a fairground mirror, magnified and distorted, until even the smallest lapse came to signal catastrophe. "They told you all that?" he said. "They had no right. That stuff's private."

"I don't give a shit about your privacy. Your daughter isn't at daycare today. You need to start thinking about that."

Over the top of the cupboard, he saw Cahill weaving through the maze of cubicles heading for his desk. He saw him rest his hands on the back of the empty chair and look around.

"Did you hear me?" Martha said.

"Are they sure she's not at daycare?"

"Of course they're bloody well sure. They sign the children in; they sign the children out. Your daughter isn't there."

He could see Cahill bent over the desk, scribbling something. "I'll ring Cathy now," he said.

"You think I haven't tried that? I've been ringing this past hour."

"She might be upstairs. She mightn't have heard the phone. Sometimes she takes her bath while Gracie's at daycare."

"I told you," Martha said—and he pictured her knuckles growing white as her grip tightened on the handset—"Gracie's not at daycare."

"I'll give it ten minutes and try her then."

"Well, let me know how you get on."

"I will," he said, "and thank you, Martha," but she had hung up.

He dialed Cathy's mobile but it went to voicemail. The landline also rang out. When he returned to his desk, the woman in the next cubicle appeared again above the partition. "Cahill," she said, nodding at a Post-it stuck to his computer screen. He peeled it off and read it. He was to bring last month's figures to the lunchtime meeting about Manchester. He crumpled the note into a ball and dropped it into the trash. He tried Cathy's number again. He thought of ringing the daycare, asking if Gracie had arrived in the meantime, but decided against it.

He took the stairs to the third floor to collect some documents, and, when he got back, he saw he had a missed call from Martha. He looked around the office. Cahill was standing a little way off, talking to one of the IT people. He went back out to the lobby and dialed Martha's number and, when she didn't answer, Cathy's. When there was still no reply, he returned to his desk, took his jacket from the back of his chair, and left the office.

He drove out of the city, past tourists shivering around the war memorial statue, past the park where mothers in hats and scarves chatted over buggies, and took the exit for the dual carriageway. Shortly after he turned onto the river road, Martha rang but the line was patchy, interspersed with bursts of static, and then there was nothing. It was not raining, but drops from overhead branches fell in an insistent patter upon the windscreen. Nature had swung on its hinges: The thaw had started, and once it had started there was nothing that could stop it. Frost was melting from the trees along the riverbank, revealing strips of torn plastic and other debris wound around their trunks in times of flood. There had been an unsilvering: The whiteness had receded, leaving soiled browns, mildewed greens. From a low-lying branch, a plastic bag hung heavy with river water. He remembered a summer at his grandparents' farm as a child, when he had found a bag, a knotted pouch of water, by the edge of a stream. Opening it, he had discovered half a dozen slimy, hairless pups, their eyes tight shut.

THERE WAS AN INCIDENT the previous November that he had kept from Martha. Cathy, he guessed, had kept it from her, too, because if Martha knew, Cathy and Gracie would be living in Castleisland now, and he would be living by himself in the house above the river. He had arrived home one evening to find the front door open, leaves blowing about the hall. "Cathy?" he called, putting down his briefcase. In the kitchen, a bag of flour had been pulled from a cupboard and upended. Gracie was under the table in just a nappy, digging jam from a jar with a fork and smearing it on the floor. She was utterly absorbed, the kitchen quiet apart from the sound of the fork striking the tiles. It was only when she looked up and saw him that she began to bawl. "Where's Mummy?" he tried, picking her up and going from room to room, but she had only cried louder.

He dressed her in clothes pulled from the laundry basket, and got a flashlight from under the stairs. Cathy's phone was on top of the kitchen table, her car parked in the driveway. He searched the garden first, quickly, because he did not expect to find Cathy there. The shed, when he checked it, was padlocked on the outside as usual. Gracie had stopped crying, distracted by the novelty of being outdoors in the dark. She waddled ahead of him, chasing the flashlight's circle of light, jumping on it, shrieking when it slid from under her feet. He climbed over the ditch into the farm next door, lifting Gracie in after him. He hoisted her onto his shoulders, steadying her with one hand, his other hand sweeping the flashlight across the shadowy grass as they made their way from field to field.

From the farm, they crossed the road to the stretch of marshy ground beside the river. The countryside at night was a different creature, the soft ground sucking at their shoes, the air thick with midges. As they got closer to the river, he noticed movement ahead, black, lumbering shapes at the edge of the trees. It was a herd of cattle, the white patches of their hides emerging like apparitions from the darkness. They were gathered in a circle, heads dipped low, steam billowing from their noses. "Moo!" Gracie shouted. "Moo! Moo!" and they stumbled apart to reveal Cathy sitting on a metal feeding trough, the ground all around her pulped muddy by hooves. She was dressed in a skirt, a short-sleeved blouse, and slippers, and when he got nearer he saw that her arms and legs were torn by briars and she was bleeding from a cut on her ankle. She looked up at him and then she looked away. Later that night, after he had bathed her and dabbed antiseptic on her cuts, after he had put her to bed and placed Gracie, sleeping, in the crook of her arm, still she wouldn't look at him.

PASSING THROUGH LINDON'S CROSS, the car slid and crossed the center line before he managed to right it again.

A heron spread its wings and rose up, flying low through the trees, toward the road. It flew so close he feared it might strike the windscreen, but it rose higher and for a moment flew ahead of the car, a silent outrider, before rising higher again, higher than seemed plausible for such a large bird, and disappearing behind a copse of trees. He touched a hand to his face and realized that he was crying. If he got home and they were safe, he would never leave them again. He would stay with them. He would not go to the office, and Cahill could do what he liked. It didn't matter anymore what Cahill thought or didn't think; it was impossible to imagine anything that mattered less than Cahill. They would manage. He would find a way. He would talk to Martha.

When he turned into the driveway, he saw that the ground surrounding the pond had been disturbed. Sods of red clay had been hacked from the lawn, their scalps of white grass run through with blades of green. A number of wooden posts had been brought from the shed and lay in a pile beside a pickax and a roll of wire mesh left behind by the builder. He stopped the car and got out. The pond itself was a mess of earth and grass, too muddied to allow sight of any fish. Part of the concrete surround was cracked, the ground beside it swampy where the water was slowly seeping away. He looked toward the house and realized that Cathy's car was missing.

He became conscious of the sound of his own breathing, of the ticks and shudders of the settling car engine. He had the sensation of being underwater, of straining against some vast, sucking tide. And then Gracie came barreling around the corner of the house. She made her way across the lawn, slipping on the wet grass, falling, getting up again. She was wearing a red dress with pink puffy sleeves, the belt flapping around her, and her Tinker Bell sandals. He ran to her and swung her up into his arms, this child he had driven away from this morning, this child he was entrusted to protect from everything and everyone. He clasped her tight, so tight that her chatter was muffled against his shirt. When he lifted his cheek from her hair, he saw Cathy walking up the garden toward them. She was carrying one of Gracie's sandals that had come off when she fell.

"Why are you home?" she said. She was wearing Wellington boots and a dress she had bought for a cousin's wedding the year before, a summer dress in flimsy material patterned in blue and yellow parrots. He saw how much looser it hung on her now, how her collarbone pressed sharply against her skin, as if it might break through.

"I forgot a file," he said.

"What a day for it to happen," she said, "with the roads so bad. We didn't even go to daycare, did we, Gracie? We went to the end of the lane and turned back."

"Where's your car?"

She was easing the sandal back on her daughter's foot, fastening the strap. "It's round the back by the shed. I was using it to move the posts. They were too heavy to carry."

Gracie wriggled out of his arms and went over to the pond. "Poor fishy," she said. She knelt on the concrete surround and dipped her arm in the water, wetting the sleeve of her dress to the shoulder. She lifted out a dead gray fish. Holding it by the tail, she swung it back and forth like a pendulum.

"That damn bird again," Cathy said. She took the fish from her daughter and laid it down on the grass. "We saw him through the window and ran out." She pointed to a gash in the fish's neck, just below the gills. "He dropped it, but we were too late. Two more are missing. Maybe three."

"Bad birdie," Gracie said. "Bad, bad birdie," and she stamped her foot.

He wanted to say that it was winter, that the bird was only doing what it always did, what it had to do. That there had never been any hope for those unwitting koi, here in this desolate place where even the river fish struggled to survive. Cathy picked up the ax. "What are you doing?" he said.

"We're going to keep the fish safe. We're going to build them a cage, like in the zoo. Right, Gracie?" When she brought the ax down, the end lodged in the lawn and she leaned on the handle, worked it like a lever, until another sod broke away. She flipped it over to reveal a tangle of roots on the underside. She was not wearing a coat or even a cardigan and her arms were purple and goosebumped. So, too, were Gracie's, he realized. The hem of her dress had trailed in the pond and the wet was soaking upward.

"Let's leave it awhile and go inside," he said.

Cathy stopped hacking at the lawn. He saw how she was looking at him, confusion in her face, trying to work out if she had displeased him. "It's okay," he said. "It's cold, that's all. We can see about it later." He took Gracie by the hand and began to walk toward the house, Cathy at his side.

"I rang earlier," he said. "I tried a few times."

"Did you? We've been out here most of the morning, haven't we, Gracie?"

Gracie nodded solemnly at her mother. "Poor fishy," she said again.

At the front door, Cathy took off her boots, left them on the step. "I've been thinking," she said, "about the daycare. It's a lot of money for Martha to come up with every month. And we don't really need it anymore, do we? I mean, I'm fine now. I can manage." She ruffled her daughter's hair. "We had fun this morning, didn't we? Just Mummy and Gracie?"

"We don't need to decide about the daycare now," he said. "We'll talk about it over the weekend."

Inside the house, Gracie toddled down the hall after her mother. He glanced at his watch, saw that the Manchester meeting was about to start.

"You might as well stay for lunch now that you're here," Cathy said.

"Sure," he said. "Why not?"

Upstairs in their bedroom, he took off his jacket and threw it on the bed. In the en suite bathroom, he opened the cabinet and took out the box containing Cathy's medication. He counted the pills in their blister pack: exactly the right number, neither too many, nor too few. He splashed water on his face and lay for a while on the bed with his eyes closed. In the inside pocket of his jacket, his phone beeped. He had three messages: a text from the in-house travel department, with booking references for flights and hotels, three nights in Manchester and then—something that had not been mentioned previously—two in Birmingham; a brusque voicemail from Martha, saying she was on her way to check on Cathy; and one from Cahill, asking where the hell he was. He switched off the phone, put it back in his jacket pocket, and went downstairs.

In the kitchen, Cathy was frying onions and cubes of bacon in a pan. "I thought we'd have omelets," she said. "Something quick, so you can get back to the office." She stood Gracie on a stool beside her and rolled up the child's sleeves. He watched Gracie smash an egg against the edge of the bowl. Half of it slipped over the rim onto the countertop, the rest, studded with fragments of shell, slid into the bowl. Cathy dipped a finger into the raw egg, fished out shards of shell. There was a determined cheerfulness to the way she moved between stove and cupboard, gathering ingredients, a grim precision to the way she chopped another onion. He noticed that she had applied lipstick while he was upstairs, and her hair was brushed. "Why don't we eat in the dining room for a change?" she said. "Gracie's going to help me set the table, aren't you, Gracie?" And she lifted the child down from the stool and led her away by the hand.

He stayed by himself in the kitchen, keeping an eye on the omelets, every so often shaking the pan to stop them catching. Through the window, he saw the frost retreating toward the mountains to the west, remnants of it forming an erratic patchwork on the bonnet of Cathy's car outside the shed. After a few moments, he took the pan off the heat and went to the door of the dining room, a rarely used room on the other side of the hall.

Cathy was at the end of the table, bent over a large silver tray. It was something they had found in a market in Dublin before they married, and it held items of crystal they had received as wedding presents. Cathy picked up a glass, held it to the light, ran a finger along the rim to check for cracks. She polished it with a tea towel, then set it down on the table and took up another. Gracie was arranging red table napkins, folding them and folding them again, pressing them down, protesting as they sprung open when released. Cathy looked up and smiled. "I thought we'd open a bottle of wine," she said. "You could have a glass with your lunch. One glass won't make any difference."

"I guess not," he said. Through the dining room window, he saw Martha's silver Volvo turn into the driveway. It came to a halt by the ruined pond, and he watched as Martha rolled down the window and stared for a while before continuing on toward the house. "What a lovely surprise," Cathy said. "And she's just in time for lunch." She left the crystal and went past him into the hall to welcome her sister.

Gracie, finished with the napkins, slid down from her chair. She was looking not at her father but about the room, ready for whatever opportunity might next present itself. There was a determined jut to her chin that didn't come from his side of the family and that always reminded him not so much of Cathy but of Martha. She headed now, with purpose, toward the tray of crystal. In an instant, she had reached up a small hand and grabbed the corner of a linen napkin on which rested a tall decanter in blue cut glass. She tugged at the napkin, and the decanter, unbalanced, began to topple sideways. "Gracie!" he heard Martha shout from behind him. But he was watching, as he was always watching, and he was there, just in time to catch it before it fell.

NIGHT OF THE SILVER FOX

———

THEY STOPPED FOR DIESEL AT A FILLING STATION OUT-side Abbeyfeale. It was late evening, dusk closing like a fist around two pumps set in a patch of rough concrete and a row of leafless poplars that bordered the forecourt. Kavanagh swung down out of the cab and slapped the flank of the lorry as if it were an animal. He was a red-faced, stocky man in his late thirties. As a child he had been nicknamed "Curly" because of his corkscrew hair, and the name had stuck, even though he was now almost entirely bald, just a patch of soft fuzz above each ear.

There was a shop with faded HB ice cream posters in the window and boxes of cornflakes on display alongside tubs of Swarfega and rat pellets. "Fill her up," Kavanagh said to the teenager who appeared in the doorway. Then

he spat on the ground and walked around the back of the
building to the toilet.

Gerard stayed in the cab and watched the boy, who was
about his own age, pump the diesel. The boy was standing
well back from the lorry, one hand holding the nozzle, the
other clamped over his nose and mouth. When his eyes met
Gerard's in the side mirror, Gerard looked away.

Three months in and he was still not used to the smell.
The fish heads with their dull, glassy eyes; the skin and scales
that stuck to his fingers; the red and purple guts that slipped
from the fishes' bellies. The smell of dead fish rose, ghost-
like, from the meal that poured into the factory silos. Gerard
shaved his hair tight, cut his nails so short his fingers bled.
At night in the pubs in Castletownbere, he imagined fine
shards of fish bone lodged like shrapnel beneath his skin,
and tiny particles of scales hanging in the air like dust motes.
The smell didn't bother Kavanagh, but then Kavanagh had
been reared to it.

"Daylight robbery," Kavanagh said when he returned to
the lorry. He handed the pump attendant the money. "Bring
me out two packets of Tayto and have a packet for yourself."
He shook his head as he climbed back into the cab. "Daylight robbery," he said again. "Four cents a liter dearer than
Slattery's."

Gerard didn't ask why they hadn't gone to Slattery's. Slattery's had stopped their tab a few weeks back, and Kavanagh
had been keeping his distance since.

Kavanagh hummed tunelessly while he waited for the

boy to return with the crisps and his change. It was a fragment of a ballad he had taken up sometime after they passed
Gurrane, forty miles earlier, and he had not let it go since.
Taped to the walls of the cab were pictures torn from magazines of women in an assortment of poses. They were mostly
Asian and in varying states of undress: Kavanagh had a thing
for Asian women. A photograph of Kavanagh's wife, Nora,
taken at last year's GAA dinner dance, was stuck between a
topless girl on a Harley-Davidson and two dark-eyed women
in crotchless panties. Nora had blond wispy hair and glasses,
and the straps of her dress dug furrows into her plump
shoulders.

"We're in Injun territory now," Kavanagh said when he
saw the boy coming across the forecourt. "These Limerick bastards would rob the teeth out of your head," and he
counted the change down to the last cent before putting it
in his pocket.

It was almost dark when they pulled back onto the road.
Kavanagh threw a packet of crisps across the cab. "That'll
keep you going," he said. "We can't count on Liddy for
grub." Four miles before Kilcroghan, they turned down a
narrow side road, grass growing up the center. Briars tore at
the sides of the lorry. "There's a man in Dundalk runs one of
these on vegetable oil," Kavanagh said. "Did you ever hear
anything about that?"

"No," said Gerard, although he remembered reading
something in a newspaper a couple of months back. If he let
on that he knew anything at all, Kavanagh would have him

tormented. Kavanagh had a child's wonder for the new and the strange. Each new fact was seized upon and dismantled, taken apart like an engine and studied in its various components. He had been bright at school but had left at fourteen to work in the fish factory.

Kavanagh shook his head. "I don't think I could stand it," he said. "The smell. It must be like driving around in a fucking chipper." Gerard glanced across at Kavanagh and tried to work out if he was serious. Kavanagh was watching the road, fingers drumming the steering wheel, humming to himself again. The light from the dashboard lent a vaguely sainted glow to his features. Gerard decided not to say anything. Kavanagh broke off his humming and sighed. "You're all chat this evening," he said. "I can't get a word in edgewise. Are you in love or what?"

"Fuck off," Gerard said, but he was smiling as he turned to look out at the trees that reached black and tall from the hedges, their branches slapping against the lorry's window.

Gerard had first been to Liddy's mink farm back in August, six weeks after he started working for Kavanagh. He had not been able to shake the memory of the place since. It was partly the farm itself and it was partly Liddy's daughter. She was about seventeen with blue-black hair, eyes heavily ringed with black liner. When Kavanagh had gone inside with her father, she had taken Gerard across the yard to show him the mink.

The mink were housed in sheds a couple of hundred feet long, twenty or thirty feet wide, with low, sloping roofs of galvanized sheeting. The sides were open to the elements, wind blowing in from the mountains to the west. Gerard followed the girl into the first shed and along a sawdust path down the center. In wire-mesh cages on either side were thousands of mink, mostly all white, with here and there a brown one. They darted back and forth and stood on their hind legs, heads weaving, snouts pressed against the wire. Their eyes glittered like wet beads, and they twisted and looped, twisted and looped, hurling their bodies against the sides of the cages.

Gerard stood in front of a cage and poked a finger through the mesh. A mink stopped chewing its fur and looked at him, a vicious tilt to its chin. It sniffed the air, crept closer, and snapped, grazing the tip of his finger. Then it backed away to stare at him from a distance.

The girl was a couple of paces ahead, watching. "I suppose you think it's cruel," she said. Her hair was tucked into the hood of her jacket, and she had her arms folded across her chest.

Gerard examined his finger and shrugged. "It's none of my business," he said.

The girl had stared at him for a moment, saying nothing, her dark eyes narrowing. Then she sighed. "It's what they're bred for," she said, turning away. "They don't know any different."

It was dark when Kavanagh swung the lorry through a muddy entrance with rough concrete pillars on either side. The lorry lurched along an uneven track, lined with chain-link fencing. In the distance, Gerard could make out the long, dark rows of the mink sheds, moonlight glinting on the metal roofs, and beyond them a huddle of outbuildings. "Liddy hasn't paid since June," Kavanagh said, "so he'll need to come up with the cash tonight. I'll sort you out then."

"It's all right," Gerard said. "It's grand," although it wasn't all right anymore. Kavanagh hadn't paid him in three weeks, and on his last visit home Gerard had to borrow from his father to pay the rent. "I'll sort you out," Kavanagh repeated as the lorry turned into the yard.

The farmhouse was a square two-story building, its whitewash fading, weeds growing from crevices in the front steps. A cat ran across the lorry's path and hid behind a row of tar barrels. Liddy's mud-spattered Jeep was parked in the yard, a back light broken. "It would be easy to feel sorry for Liddy," Kavanagh said, "but what would be the use in that?" and they both got out of the lorry.

A light came on in the porch and Liddy himself appeared. He was a stooped, wiry man, a gray cardigan hanging loose from his shoulders, and his eyes darted from Kavanagh to Gerard and back again as he came toward them across the yard. His skin had the waxy, pinched look of a museum doll. It reminded Gerard of how his mother had looked in the months before she died, and he knew immediately that Liddy was sick.

"How're the men?" Liddy held out a bony hand to Kavanagh, who took it in his own vast paw and squeezed until Gerard expected to hear bones crack. Liddy's daughter had come out onto the porch. She was slouched against the doorframe, arms folded, her black hair pulled loosely into a ponytail.

Liddy looked up at the night sky with its shifting mass of cloud. "The rain will be on soon," he said. "You might as well get her unloaded. I'll put the kettle on for tea."

Gerard went to release the back of the lorry, but Kavanagh held up a hand. "Hold on a minute," he said. "If it was tea I was after I could have stayed at home. Tea is fuck all use to me."

The girl, wearing tracksuit bottoms and a vest, was coming down the porch steps and across the yard. She had the same black-ringed eyes that Gerard remembered from before.

Liddy had already begun to shuffle toward the house. He called back over his shoulder to Kavanagh. "Don't you know I'm good for it?" he said. "Have I ever let you down yet?"

Kavanagh didn't budge. "That's three loads you owe me now," he said. "I've bills to pay. I've this young fella here to pay." He nodded at Gerard, who stood waiting by the lorry.

Liddy stopped. He gave a wheeze that shook his chest and caused him to bend almost double, hands on his knees. "Sure, what could a young lad like that want?" he said, when he righted himself again. "A young lad like that would be happy sitting under a bush with a can." He laughed then, but Kavanagh didn't.

"Leave it, for the time being." It was the girl, her voice

slightly muzzy as if she had been sleeping. She raised both hands behind her head and stretched like a cat. "We can talk about it inside." She turned and walked toward the house, and the three men followed.

The porch was stacked with bags of coal and kindling. A plastic bucket and a broom stood in one corner beside two pairs of Wellington boots caked with mud and sawdust. A picture of Pope John Paul II, arms outstretched, hung next to a calendar from the Fortrush Fisherman's Co-op, two years out of date, days circled and crossed in spidery ink. Beyond the porch was a dark, narrow hallway. Liddy faltered, but the girl pushed open a door into a small sitting room.

There was a mahogany chest of drawers with ornate carvings that must have come from a bigger, grander house. Squares of faded linen were folded on top, next to a family of blue china elephants. The room smelled of things put away, of dust laid down on dust. The carpet was brown with an orange fleck, and along one wall was a sofa in a dull mustard color. On either side of the fireplace were two matching armchairs, their plastic covers still in place. A copy of the *Fur Farmers' Yearbook* and a few tatty paperbacks sat on a coffee table.

Liddy took one armchair, Kavanagh the other. As he lowered himself onto the sofa, Gerard caught a glimpse of himself in a mirror above the fireplace. His skin was still lightly tanned from days spent on the pier over the summer. His shorn hair carried a hint of menace to which he had not yet grown accustomed. He took off his jacket and placed it beside him on the sofa, and as he did so he thought that he caught a faint odor of dead fish. Through the open curtains, he saw the moon reflecting in the puddles that lay like small lakes upon the surface of the yard.

"You'll have a drop of something?" The girl spoke like a woman twice her age. Standing there, waiting for an answer, she could have been the woman, not just of the house, but of the farm and the yard, the dark rows of mink sheds, and the wet fields and ditches out beyond.

Kavanagh shook his head. "Tea's grand," he said.

Her eyes settled next on Gerard, who felt his face grow red.

Kavanagh looked across and chuckled. "He's the strong, silent type," he said. "He has the women of Castletown-bere driven half-mad." He winked at the girl. "You could do worse."

The girl, momentarily shy, gazed at the carpet and tucked a wisp of hair behind one ear. "Tea's fine," Gerard said, and the girl smiled at him before going out of the room.

After she had gone, the men sat in silence. Kavanagh was never short of something to say, and Gerard knew the silence was a shot across the bow: Kavanagh's way of sending a message to Liddy.

Liddy stared into the empty grate for a while and then, when there was still nothing from Kavanagh, he addressed himself instead to Gerard. "What part of the country are you from, yourself?" he said. "And through what misfortune did you end up with this latchico?"

Gerard was a second cousin of Kavanagh's on his mother's side, and Kavanagh had taken him on at the fish factory after he finished school that summer. It was partly Kavanagh's way of looking out for the boy after the death of Gerard's mother the year before. It was also because Gerard's father had lent Kavanagh the money to fix the factory roof after the storms the previous winter, and Kavanagh had yet to repay him.

Gerard could feel Liddy's eyes on him, waiting for an answer. He was saved by Kavanagh breaking his silence. "Isn't he the lucky boy to have a job at all?" he said. "Every other lad his age is in Australia."

"Luck is a two-faced whore," Liddy said. "There's people said I was lucky when I got this place."

Kavanagh fell quiet and when he spoke again it was to inquire after a relative of Liddy's who was in the hospital at Croom. The talk turned next to football and greyhounds and, for a while, a peace of sorts settled on the room.

When the girl came back with the tea she had changed into a low-cut pink top and a short black skirt that clung to her hips and thighs. Her hair, freshly brushed and more indigo than black, hung past her shoulders. She was carrying a tray with the tea and a plate of Club Milks, and as she bent to set it down on the coffee table Gerard's eyes went to her plump, white breasts and slid into the valley between them. The girl was putting cups in saucers, pouring tea. Without warning she raised her head and caught him looking. She stared at him until, blushing, he returned the stare, and he noticed for the first time that her eyes, which he had thought were brown, were in fact a very dark blue, almost navy. Then she straightened up, tucked the empty tray under her arm, and went out of the room.

Kavanagh unwrapped a Club Milk, took half of it into his mouth in one bite, and chewed slowly. "Well, Liddy," he said. "What have you got for me?"

Liddy leaned forward in his chair. "We had the activists a while back," he said. "Ten minutes with a wire cutter and I'm down a thousand mink. Next morning, I've a farmer at my door with a trailer full of dead lambs, all with holes in their throats." Liddy shook his head and brought a hand to his own thin throat.

"Those fuckers should be shot," Kavanagh said. "Thundering bastards. I know what I'd do with their wire cutters."

Liddy's hand left his throat and settled instead on his knee, which immediately began to jig. "We had a cull last month: Aleutian disease."

Kavanagh sighed and put his cup down heavily on the table. "Listen," he said. "Do I look like Mother Teresa? There isn't any of us has it easy."

"If I'd known what I was letting myself in for," Liddy said, "I'd never have come out here." He seemed to be talking more to himself than to Kavanagh. "I'd have stayed in the city and saved myself a lot of trouble."

"Trouble knows its way around," Kavanagh said. "I've the bank on my case, I've the wife on my case, and I've this young fellow here to pay." He pointed to the pile of Club

Milk wrappers that had accumulated in front of Gerard. "Look at him; he's half-starved."

Apart from the crisps in the lorry earlier, Gerard hadn't eaten anything since they had left Castletownbere shortly after four o'clock. He was about to open another Club Milk, but now he put it back on the plate.

"I'll have it in a lump sum next time," Liddy said.

"You'll have it tonight, or I'll turn that lorry around and drive back the way I came."

"I've a man coming for pelts on Tuesday. Call in the next time you're passing."

A flush was edging up Kavanagh's neck, spreading over his cheeks. "There's nothing for nothing in this world," he said. "You can pay me tonight or you can go to hell."

"I wouldn't have to go far," Liddy said. "Look around you."

A sullenness had come over Liddy. The forced banter of earlier had disappeared and in its place was a sour obstinacy that hardened into bitter lines around his mouth. Gerard had a sudden vision of how Liddy would look laid out: his body sunken in a too-big suit, a tie awkward at his throat, even the silk lining of the coffin pressing heavy on his arms.

There was a noise outside in the yard; the clank of metal on concrete. Kavanagh was first to his feet, the others following behind. The girl was on a forklift. She wore no helmet, and the wind that blew across the yard snatched at her hair, snaking it in black tails about her face. She had released the back of the lorry and was unloading a pallet of fish meal.

Kavanagh crossed the yard like a bull. The girl stopped the forklift but didn't get out. Her face was pale in the light of the porch lamp. "Fucking cunt," Kavanagh was roaring, and he started to swing bags of meal from the forklift like they were cotton candy. Liddy watched from a distance. Gerard went to help, but the girl had been intercepted early and already everything was back on the lorry. "I thought I'd make a start," she said. "It's getting late."

"Do you think I'm some class of fool?" Kavanagh said.

The girl's voice was soft, measured, as if calming a small child. "You're no fool, Curly," she said. "Come here and talk to me." She patted the passenger seat of the forklift. Kavanagh looked away and shook his head. "I've enough time wasted," he said, and began to walk toward the lorry.

The girl called after him. "Hey, Curly," she said. "Don't be like that." Her voice dropped lower. "You can't go yet. You haven't seen the silver foxes." She was leaning out of the forklift, her shadow stretching across the yard. "We brought them over from England last month. They're still only cubs." She was looking directly at Kavanagh, her head tilted slightly to one side, her lips parted. "Come down to the shed and I'll show you. You've never seen foxes like these."

Kavanagh had reached the door of the cab. He stopped, one foot on the step. In the forklift, the girl patted the passenger seat again and winked. Kavanagh appeared to be considering. Liddy was standing by himself, staring at the ground. For a while everything was very still, and there was only the sound of the wind rattling across the roofs of the mink sheds and the cry of a small animal in the trees beyond. Then Kavanagh strode across the yard to the forklift and climbed in. They drove off, the girl at the wheel, the wind whipping up her dark hair, Kavanagh bald and stocky in the seat beside her. The forklift went to the far end of the yard and disappeared behind some outbuildings.

Gerard and Liddy were left standing in the yard. Liddy looked like a man who had been struck. He did nothing for a moment, then turned and began his stooped walk back to the house. Gerard was about to go to the lorry and wait when Liddy shouted to him from the porch. "You might as well come in," he said.

This time, instead of going into the sitting room, they continued down the hall and into a small wood-paneled kitchen. A table and two chairs were pushed tight against one wall, a stove, a sink, and an assortment of mismatched kitchen units against another. There was a wooden dresser stacked with old newspapers and chipped crockery. The stale grease of a fry hung in the air. To one side of the back door, in a glass display cabinet, was a stuffed brown mink. It was mounted on a marble base on which was inscribed something Gerard could not read. The mink stood on its hind legs, teeth bared in a rigid grin, front legs clawing the air.

Liddy took a bottle of whiskey from a cupboard beneath the sink and wiped two glasses on the end of his cardigan. He sat at the table and gestured at Gerard to sit beside him.

"She's gone five years now," Liddy said, pouring the whis-

key. Gerard didn't understand at first. He had been thinking of the girl behind the outbuildings with Kavanagh. The
white breasts, the dark eyes. Her mouth, wide and loose;
her red lips and a stud on her tongue that had flashed silver
when she smiled at something earlier in the evening. Then
he realized Liddy was staring at a photograph high on the
wall above the dresser. It was of a woman, tall and angular,
with straight brown hair, her hand resting on the shoulder
of a girl in a Communion dress. "I'm sorry," Gerard said,
because he couldn't think of anything else to say and it was
what people had said when his mother died.

"Oh, I'm not sorry," Liddy said, throwing back his whiskey and pouring another. "There's a lot I'm sorry about, but
not that." His weariness had been replaced with anger. "She
took herself off to Belfast. She told me she was going to stay
with her sister, but you can be sure she had a man waiting.
It was always the same with that woman: She'd tell you that
day was night." His head jutted forward and Gerard smelled
the sourness of his breath. "I asked her to take the girl with
her," Liddy said, "but she wouldn't." He put down his glass
and spread his hands wide, palms upward, in supplication.
"What sort of life is it for a young girl out here, I asked her,
but she left us to it, Rosie and myself."

Rosie. The girl's name didn't suit her, Gerard thought. It
was too tame, too domesticated. It was a name for a spoiled
poodle in a wicker basket, not a girl with a tongue piercing
who could drive a forklift. Liddy drank more whiskey. "Rosie

was twelve when she left," he said, "and what did I know about raising a child? A girl needs her mother. Boys are different. Boys can make their way, but girls need mothers."

Liddy fell silent, swirled whiskey around the end of his glass. Gerard wanted to get up and leave but he knew that he could not. It was a moment before Liddy spoke again. "It was coming out here did it," he said. "She was always a flighty woman. She had one eye on the door from the day I married her, but we got along well enough up to that. A couple of winters here and nothing could hold her."

Liddy was becoming more and more agitated, his hands moving incessantly, almost knocking over his glass. Gerard's own glass was barely touched. He thought of Kavanagh and the girl in the shadows of the outbuildings. He wondered if silver foxes were the same as ordinary foxes, only silver, or if they were some different creature entirely, and then he wondered if there were any silver foxes at all. He imagined the cubs in Kavanagh's rough hands and Kavanagh, awed and silent, turning them this way and that.

"Her mother, bitch and all that she is, would make a better hand of her," Liddy said. "Rosie's a good girl, a fighter, but what chance has a girl out here?"

Gerard knew that he should say something but had no idea what.

"Rosie will be okay," he said. "Rosie's a smart girl."

Liddy stared at him, his eyes bloodshot. All of the anger left him and he sagged over the table. "She is," he said. "She's a smart girl. And a good girl."

He set his glass down on the table and buried his head in his arms. The kitchen was utterly quiet, nothing but the sound of the wind whistling under the back door. A strange sound came from Liddy, half cough, half sob. Then another that caught and lengthened until it became a wail. Liddy was crying, his shoulders quivering, the top of his head shaking. Gerard took a mouthful of whiskey, felt it burn the pit of his stomach. Liddy was bawling now, his head still in his arms. Gerard pushed his chair back and stood up. He went over to the sink and placed his glass on the draining board. He took one last look at Liddy crumpled over the table, then left the kitchen and went back down the narrow hall and outside to the yard.

When he got to the lorry, he discovered that Kavanagh had locked it and taken the key. The night had grown colder. Gerard remembered his jacket, still in the sitting room where he had left it earlier, but he thought of Liddy weeping inside the house and decided to do without. A light was on in a prefab, but the door, when he tried it, was padlocked. He took shelter instead beneath the overhang of the prefab's roof, next to a row of barrels. He wrapped his arms around himself and hoped that Kavanagh would not be long. Something warm brushed against his legs, and he saw a cat dart from behind a barrel and streak across the yard.

He pressed his face against the prefab window. The walls were hung with pelts: thousands of headless, bodiless furs, their arms spread wide and pinned to wooden racks. On a bench was a machine with long silver-toothed blades and, beside it, a pile of dead mink. He noticed a smell coming from the barrel nearest him and lifted the lid. Inside were the skinned corpses of the mink, pink and slippery and hairless. He dropped the lid of the barrel and stepped back from the window.

The wind carried fragments of laughter up the yard and he saw Kavanagh and the girl returning on the forklift. This time Kavanagh was driving, the girl beside him, an arm flung across his shoulder. They slowed as they passed the pelt shed and waved. Gerard stepped out from the shelter of the building and walked behind the forklift to the lorry. A drizzle blew in from the mountains, stinging his face. Kavanagh, flushed and sweating, jumped out of the forklift. "Give us a hand," he said to Gerard without looking at him, and together they began to unload the lorry. Gerard shivered in his shirtsleeves, but the cold, like the smell, didn't seem to bother Kavanagh.

Gerard felt someone touch his arm. The girl was behind him, holding his jacket. She didn't say a word, but Gerard held out his arms and allowed her to slip the jacket on, let her zip it up and smooth it down over his shoulders.

Afterward, as they turned the lorry in the yard, Gerard noticed Liddy standing alone on the porch. Gerard raised a hand and waved, but Liddy didn't wave back. The girl was by the forklift, hands in her pockets. Gerard watched her in the rearview mirror as the lorry drove out of the yard, saw her turn and walk toward the house, saw the light go out on the porch.

Kavanagh didn't speak until they reached the end of the muddy track and were back on the road. "I'm calling on Clancy tomorrow," he said. "He owes me a few bob. I'll sort you out then."

"It's all right," Gerard said.

They drove in silence for a while, the only sound the relentless squeak of the wipers as the rain grew heavier. "Tell me," Kavanagh said. "Did you ever see a silver fox?" Gerard shook his head. Kavanagh let out a low whistle. "Beautiful animals," he said. "Beautiful. But why do you think their fur is that color? Aren't they foxes, at the end of the day?"

Gerard shrugged and looked out the window. Kavanagh kept talking, his voice becoming more animated, his hands restless on the steering wheel. "They weren't silver, exactly," he said. "You'd be expecting silver but it was more . . ." He paused, and his eyes scanned the cab—his wife's photograph, the pictures of the Asian women, the collection of knickknacks on the dash. When his surroundings failed him, he clicked his tongue in exasperation. "They were a sort of bluey black," he said. "White bits on their tails and faces. Little balls of fur." He went suddenly quiet, as if he had embarrassed himself.

Back on the main road, the lorry picked up speed as they headed south. A few miles on, Kavanagh spoke again. "What kind of life is it at all?" he said. "Weaned at six weeks and shipped off in a crate?"

It was cold in the cab, and Gerard pulled his jacket tighter around him. He put a hand to the inside pocket, felt for his wallet, and realized that it was gone. Shadowy trees and ditches blurred past. The wind blew dark, shapeless things across the path of the lorry, things that might have been alive or might have been dead: tiny night creatures and flurries of fallen leaves. They drove on through small, half-lit towns, through dark countryside whose only light was the flicker of wide-screen televisions in bungalow windows. Kavanagh began to hum. It was the chorus of a country and western song, full of love and violence, and he kept it up until they reached Bantry and took the dark coast road for Castletownbere.

NOT OLEANDERS

———

THE TRAIN STOPPED AT A STATION EAST OF ROME, a
small, bucolic station with tomatoes stacked high in wooden
crates. The doors opened and an odd rancid smell rushed
the carriage, hot and sweaty and carnal, like meat on the
point of turning. The young Austrian woman sitting across
from Lily noticed it, too. She looked up from her notebook
and frowned, the same quizzical, slightly nervous frown
she'd presented to the ticket checker earlier, even though
she had a ticket, had it ready for inspection since the train
pulled out of Termini.

"Oleanders," Lily said. She'd seen them growing along
the edge of the railway line as the train wheezed into the station, a profusion of white-flowering bushes depositing petals
onto the tracks. The Austrian woman smiled and looked re-

lieved, as if the smell had sent her mind down a siding filled with other things, things darker and unflowery.

Her name was Etta, and she was traveling to Gariano, where she would spend two weeks. She'd laughed, but not in an unkind way, at something Lily said about Sacher torte, and when Lily had mentioned that she'd nothing to read, Etta had given her a book—a French novel in translation—and told her to keep it. She was in her midtwenties, a doctoral student in geothermal energy, something she'd spoken about fervently before they'd moved to the more manageable topic of Italian rail timetables. She closed her notebook now and put it in one of the myriad zipped pockets of her holdall. At every stop along the route, at every tiny backwater, she'd taken out the notebook and copied down the name of the station in tiny, neat handwriting, as if they were pebbles she might need to find her way back.

They'd fallen into conversation shortly after Peroli, the second to last stop before Rocosalto, where they were both getting out. Etta had blond hair in a ponytail and blond brows and the lightest fuzz of blond hair on her upper lip. Lily watched her take a tiny mirror from the holdall and dab at the sweat beading her hairline. Her blouse had slid off one shoulder, exposing a delicate clavicle no thicker than a chicken bone and perilously close to the surface. In the waiting room at Rocosalto, she settled herself one bench down from Lily and took out the notebook. It was unclear whether or not she desired company. Their conversation on the train, though fleeting, had been pleasant, very pleasant, but now

Lily wondered if perhaps its pleasantness might have been rooted in the very fact that it was fleeting, if perhaps she should leave well enough alone.

It was just the two of them in the waiting room, apart from a woman with a child of about three or four. The child slid from his mother's lap and, going over to the vending machine, delivered a kick to the glass front. The man behind the cashier's desk stood up—to scold the child, Lily presumed, but instead he switched the sign on the hatch from APERTO to CHIUSO and pulled shut the grille. A moment later, he came out a door in the corner of the room and, giving the barest of nods, left. The child lay on the floor and inspected the cord that ran from the machine to the wall, tugging at it, poking his fingers into the weave of exposed wires. Children were like that, Lily thought; children added to the dangers of an already dangerous world, and how was it that so few people besides her seemed to realize this? The child's mother jumped up and slapped him hard across his legs before dragging him back to their seat, where he climbed again onto her lap and began to cry softly.

Etta got up and came over. "Do you think he's coming back?" she said, inclining her head toward the cashier's window.

"I don't know," Lily said. "Do you need to buy a ticket?"

"I don't think so, but they should have somebody here, shouldn't they? And I'd like to get a map." She was frowning again, biting on her lower lip. Lily wondered if she should invite her to sit. The sweet, uncomplicated pleasure of their encounter on the train was now a hair's breadth from descending into awkwardness. If someone didn't arrive for one or other of them soon, it would be spoiled entirely. Things were very easily spoiled.

"Here," Lily said, taking out a map she'd picked up at the airport. "Have this."

Etta shook her head. "Thank you," she said, "but I have that one already. I wanted to get a different one. Perhaps he will be back." She hesitated then, and her gaze seemed to shift from Lily's face, moving higher and a little to one side. Another frown. "Keep still," she said, and she reached out, rummaged with her fingers in Lily's hair. When she withdrew her hand, she was holding a petal between thumb and forefinger, one of the gauzy oleander petals that were blowing like confetti up and down the platform and in through the door of the waiting room.

"Thank you," Lily said.

"You have very beautiful hair," Etta said. "I thought to tell you that on the train, but I didn't. Such a beautiful color, like nutmeg." And then she scuttled back to her own bench.

Rocosalto was a small, faded town, at least those parts visible from the train station: a strip of flat-roofed shop units, a couple of bars, a *tabaccheria*. Taking her suitcase with her, Lily got up and went to the door of the waiting room. Sandra, being the organized one, had booked this year's holiday immediately upon their return from last year's. She had a thing for "off the beaten track," which more often than not translated into soup in chipped bowls and bunk beds. Lily had worked out exactly what she'd say when Sandra asked for her half of the money back; she'd written it out on a piece of card. But Sandra hadn't asked.

There was a fountain in the middle of the square outside the station: three copper heads on a marble plinth. It hinted not at honor but at reprisal: decapitated heads left to bake in the sun, mouths slightly parted as if they'd cried out while the cast was being poured. Lily went over and sank her arms in the water, sluiced them back and forth, in and out around the bloated cigarette butts that floated on the surface like belly-up maggots. The water was cool, but in this position, bent over the basin, her hair fell forward onto her face and the sun scorched the back of her neck. Etta had come to stand in the doorway of the waiting room. She didn't wave or call out or inquire about the fountain. She just leaned against the doorframe, watching. *Nutmeg*. Nobody had used that word to describe her hair before, but now that she thought about it, that's exactly the color it was.

A man arrived pushing a baby in a buggy. As he squeezed past Etta, a wheel glanced against her foot, knocking off her shoe, which snagged on the undercarriage of the buggy and got carried forward a short distance. Etta hopped on one foot as she went to retrieve it, a graceful, elegant hopping, the shoeless foot raised up behind her so that she looked for all the world like a flamingo. Lily turned back to the fountain, ran a hand again through the water. She was thirty-nine, battle-scarred, fraying around the edges. The last thing she needed was some undamaged twenty-five-year-old—

anyone, for that matter, who might consider themselves entitled to beauty. She was too tired for all of that. The man
with the buggy came out of the waiting room, accompanied by the mother and child, and as they went by the baby
started up a loud wailing.

Sandra and Julie would probably have a baby. Sandra
had said as much when she'd called round last month with
the renewal forms for the parking permit, which had always
been in her name. She'd delivered the pronouncement in
small, hesitant sentences, punctuated with long pauses, as
if, already, before it was even conceived, the baby required
delicate handling. Lily couldn't give a damn about the baby
and had told her so. The baby wasn't the point. What a pity
Sandra hadn't shown such propriety in other things: who she
slept with, for example. They could have half a dozen babies
for all Lily cared; half a dozen mewling, puking, shitting babies one after the other. It was, in fact, what she wished for
them, what they both deserved.

A truck pulled into the parking lot, an open-backed
truck with one side panel a darker green than the rest and
the name of the hotel where Lily was staying emblazoned
across the bonnet. The driver, a stocky man in his forties,
jumped out. *"Ciao, bella,"* he shouted, at the same time waving across the square to Etta, beckoning her over. Etta didn't
budge, but she shifted position in the doorway, stood a little
straighter.

"It's just me," Lily said.

"No," the driver said. *"Due."* He took a piece of paper

from his shirt pocket and read out first her name, then Sandra's.

"My friend wasn't able to come," Lily said. "She's sick."

"Ah," he said. "I am sorry to hear that. Very sorry." He glanced in the direction of the waiting room. "And the young lady?"

"She's not with me."

He shrugged and seized her suitcase, threw it in the back of the truck as if it were an animal to be grappled with. He covered it with tarpaulin and tied it down with thick rope. Inside the cab, the seat was torn and speckled with ciga-rette burns. It was also tiny—how three of them might have fitted, Lily couldn't imagine. As she fastened her seatbelt, she saw Etta crossing the square to the fountain, her holdall slung across her shoulder. The driver put the truck in gear, a process that seemed to involve much brushing against Lily's leg, or was she imagining that? Etta settled herself on the edge of the fountain and drummed her heels against the marble. The cashier hadn't returned, and the buildings on either side of the station had brought their shutters down. Lily wondered if she should inquire if Etta had heard from whoever was supposed to be collecting her. They could hardly just leave her here by herself, could they? But as she was trying to work out how to roll down the cab window, the driver swung the truck in a wide, sweeping arc and drove at speed out of the station.

At the tollbooth outside town, his arm rested a mo-ment on her knee as he rooted in the ashtray for coins. Back home, she was considered pale; here, her legs appeared startlingly white, as if her entire life up to now had been lived underground. The driver, whose name was Allesandro, said something to the tollbooth operator and the operator laughed, then glanced at her as if to see how she was taking it. They were driving into lush, verdant countryside, swaths of green meadowlands checkered with squares of blazing yellow saffron. They drove up into the mountains, through pastureland thick with wildflowers, rabbles of multicolored butterflies gusting across the windscreen. Every so often, there were warnings of deer: signs depicting Lilliputian animals, fairy-sized beasts, captured mid-leap. She'd left her sunglasses in her suitcase, and even when she shut her eyes a yellow haze persisted behind her lids.

"Your friend," Allesandro said. "Is she very sick or just a little sick?"

"Very sick," Lily said. "Non-Hodgkin's lymphoma," because she'd read an article about that on the plane on the way over and, anyway, Sandra deserved it.

"Santa Madonna," Allesandro said, and he shook his head. "I am sad for you, very sad."

They turned at a sign for Rifugio del Lupo, a timber chalet-style building of a kind Lily associated not with Italy, but with Switzerland, where she'd holidayed once with Sandra. The patch of rough gravel that served as a parking lot contained just three cars. On a small terrace to the front, parasols bearing the logo of an ice-cream company shaded red plastic tables and chairs. She followed Allesandro into a dimly lit bar with benches upholstered in faded velveteen. At a table in one corner a group of four—two men and two women—were sharing a bottle of wine, though there was no sign of anybody who might have served them. Giant pine-cones painted with artificial snow hung from the ceiling, and on the shelves behind the counter were plastic reindeer, tinsel, a Nativity set, and other things out of season.

THOSE WHITE-FLOWERING, SMELLY BUSHES that grew along the railway line were not oleanders. Oleanders, it turned out, were a different creature entirely. For one thing, oleanders were biggish with dark green leaves that were long and leathery. Their five-petaled flowers stood distinctly on barky stalks. Nothing, in other words, like the messy, breathy balls of white that had graced the bushes she'd seen earlier. She knew this now because on the wall of the bedroom Allesandro showed her to there was a framed picture of flora and fauna of the region, an educational-style bilingual poster of the kind seen in interpretative centers. It had dozens of species of wildflowers and tiny field animals, hand-drawn in astonishing detail with close-ups of petals and stamen and seeds and, occasionally, as if the artist had tired of the concentrated gaze, a lake, a mountain, a rooftop panorama, dropped unceremoniously between plants and insects with no thought as to scale.

"It's good, yes?" Allesandro said, setting down her suit-case and sweeping an arm wide to encompass the room.

She didn't know what to say, because actually, if she was truthful, it wasn't. It was narrow and painted a dull mustard color, a rushed careless job because all around the edges someone—Allesandro, she guessed—had allowed the mustard to leak into the white of the ceiling. There was a bed, a wardrobe, and a sink set into a square of cracked tiles. Vintage Sandra. She looked about for a door that might lead to a bathroom, but there wasn't any. "It's lovely," she said. It wasn't a downright lie, because the view from the window was spectacular: the shadows crossing the mountainside, the colors of the sky as it slid toward evening, lights in the valley arranging themselves dot by dot into tiny villages.

After Allesandro left her to unpack, she studied the poster to see if she could establish the true identity of the pretender plants, the ones that were not oleanders, but they were nowhere to be seen. The real oleanders stared out at her reproachfully. The poster reminded her of one from boarding school, only that one had been solely in English and had featured birds instead of plants. Categories and subcategories of finches and sparrows and hawks; a grotesque side panel of mummified birds, macabre depictions of a kind no longer allowed in schools, that had flown into a poisonous lake in Tanzania mistaking it for sky. She took some wipes from her suitcase and scrubbed the sink where she'd noticed a rim of scum. She wiped the windowsill, too, and dusted the top of the bedside locker, rubbing and cursing, all the time wishing that Sandra was there. "Now," she'd say to her if she was, "now look what you've done."

❋ ❋ ❋

IN THE DINING ROOM the next morning she found the walls
hung with snow scenes, mostly of the Rifugio shot from various angles, the trees all about it dripping snow and snow
heavy on its roof. She was reminded of Victorian Christmas
cards, or a montage from the inside of a snow globe. "It must
be magnificent in wintertime," she said to Allesandro, who
arrived bearing syrupy coffee and a basket of bread. "Yes,"
he said, "very white, very beautiful." His gaze dropped to
her legs and he winked. As he moved between tables, tend-
ing to his other guests, she caught him sneaking glances.
Was it possible that she was more attractive in this country
than in her own? That desire was shaped, in part at least, by
the vagaries of geography?

She'd gone to bed early the evening before but had slept
badly, waking at three A.M. to visions of Etta, still not collected, waiting alone at the train station. She'd gotten out of
bed and gone to stand by the window, which was a mistake,
because immediately upon parting the curtains she'd seen
to the west a thick plume of yellowy white smoke billowing
from the direction of Rocosalto. She pictured Etta perched
on the fountain, frowning as the smell of burning reached
her. If Sandra were here, she'd say that this was a whole new
level of foolishness. It was arrogant in the extreme—she recalled how Sandra had called her that once, arrogant—to in-
terpret every vibration of the universe as relatable to her life,
her needs, her acts and omissions. It's not about you, Sandra

would say, which Lily had always thought particularly unfair because she never did think it was about her—it had been such a long time since anything was. Then she'd realized that she was looking east, not west, and Rocosalto was in the other direction entirely, and she had climbed back into bed and slept fitfully until dawn.

After breakfast she fetched the book Etta had given her on the train and decided she would go outside to read. It was a slim volume, barely a hundred pages, and Etta had said she thought she would like it. Stepping onto the terrace was like stepping into an oven, but the air was sweet, the scent of pine needles mingling with the smell of wildflowers, the green of the meadows gloriously ruptured with bursts of purples and yellows and blues. It was when she walked around the back of the hotel, searching for a place to sit, that she got the other smell, the fermented, sour smell from the day before. She tracked it to a copse of squat, bushy-headed trees. Figs. Not any kind of flower then, but unharvested figs left to rot where they fell. She pulled one from a branch and bit it. It was foul, bitter, and she spat it out immediately onto the ground. Beyond the fig trees, a flight of concrete steps led to a stilled ski lift, its chain of linked metal chairs disappearing up the mountainside. She climbed into one and sat facing the summit, her back to the Rifugio. She swung her legs back and forth, creating a pleasant breeze, and opened the book.

And there it was, on the title page: Ulrike Etta Dorn and a telephone number. She brought the book closer, examined the handwriting. It was scrawled, slightly jittery, as if it had been written in a hurry, and she remembered now that there had been a moment when she'd left her seat to ask the ticket checker a question. The insistence with which Etta had pressed the book upon her—please, you must have it, you must keep it—returned, as did her own shilly-shallying in the station waiting room, the rudeness of her departure. She took out her phone and dialed the number. Etta answered, eventually, in German. She sounded different in that language. "Hello," Lily said, then realized it was Etta's voicemail and hung up. She should have realized that might happen. She should have thought about what to say and written it down—hadn't she learned that the hard way with Sandra?—but she didn't have a pen. "Hello," she said next time on the beep. "I'm sorry I drove off. I hope you're all right." She began to recite her own number, but faltered, lost her place, and, unable to find her way back into the sequence, hung up again.

TWICE THE TAXI DRIVER asked her to repeat the name of the town, as if sure that he must have misheard. It was situated in what her guidebook described as a zone of light industry, down in the flat of the plain, and for "plain" read "ugly," because there were no pretty farmsteads here, no quaint goatherd huts. There were fields of solar panels, car dealerships, factories of various kinds blowing out steam. And it was much farther away than she'd thought, over an hour's drive. She speed-read the book on the way, skipping every second page. Since the likelihood was that Etta was still alive, she'd also googled "geothermal" and had memorized a few phrases. Context would be tricky, of course, she'd have to watch context, and she'd better not get things mixed up, or it would be oleanders all over again.

At the entrance to Gariano there was a crumbling stone arch that must once have formed part of the town walls, though almost nothing else of the walls remained, apart from a few freestanding banks of stone leaning toward rubble. Etta hadn't mentioned the name of her hotel, but as it turned out, there was only one, a hideous affair of modern construction halfway along the town's main street. And just as Lily finished paying the taxi driver, before he had even driven off, she saw her—Etta—at a table on the pavement. Not only was she not dead, she looked entirely well—better than well, in fact. She looked beautiful. She looked different, too, though it was difficult to say in precisely what way. More composed, perhaps, less helpless. Or had Lily just imagined the helplessness? She was writing in the same notebook as the day before, but today even the movement of her wrist seemed stronger, more assured. "Oh, hello," she said, glancing up, and she frowned, an entirely different sort of frown to the one Lily remembered from the train. "I thought you were staying in the mountains?"

"I was," Lily said. "I am. In Ovindoli."

"Isn't that very far away?"

"Yes," Lily said, "I suppose it is."

"What are you doing here?" Etta said.

"I rang," Lily said. "I tried to ring. I left a message."

"You rang the hotel?"

"No, I rang you. I left a message. Two messages."

Etta frowned again. "But how did you get my number?" She picked up a phone from beside her on the table and shook her head. "No messages," she said.

The table was in the shade of an awning, but Lily was standing in the full glare of the sun. Out of vanity, she hadn't worn a hat. She'd wanted to show off her hair—nutmeg— and now she could feel the top of her head beginning to burn. In an attempt to move things forward, she said: "I enjoyed the book very much."

"I thought you'd like it," Etta said. "I found it a little old-fashioned, but my mother loved it. I thought you might like it, too."

"I see," Lily said. The book had been bloody awful actually; she hadn't been able to make head nor tail of it. She took it from her bag now and opened it to the title page. "Anyway," she said, "that's where I got your number. And I did leave a message but—"

Etta was laughing. "Oh, that's my mother's number," she said. "She does that with all her books. Don't ask me why." She paused. "But what are you doing here?"

How to explain it, even to herself? Hope, she might have said, if she'd tried; the eternal triumph of hope over experience. That and the fact that, if she was honest, there was something about this young woman that reminded her of Sandra; she'd noticed it the minute Etta had settled into the seat opposite her on the train. Not a recent Sandra, an earlier version. She looked around to see if some plausible destination might present itself and saw an insurance office, a dry cleaners, a bank. "I came to see you," she said.

Even at this late stage, there was the possibility that something might have been saved. There could have been a visit to the stone arch where together they might have deciphered the inscription above the entrance; a coffee, perhaps, in the hotel bar. Life, after all, was mostly the art of salvage. But Etta, her expression shifting in sudden recognition, was too young yet, too undamaged, to have learned this. "Oh," she said. "I understand." And then, "I'm seeing somebody."

"Yes," Lily said. "Of course."

Then Etta set her mouth in a tight line and bent her head to her notebook. A strand of blond hair swung forward over the page like a guillotine. Today she was wearing a halter-neck top and there, again, were the beautiful clavicles: so snappable and exposed that Lily wanted to reach out and tug at the fabric in an effort to cover them, to tell this young woman who knew nothing that anything that can be seen can be broken. She stood a moment by the table, and when Etta said no more, she turned and walked to the end of the street where she could see the taxi driver buying cigarettes at a kiosk. Less than five minutes had passed since he'd dropped her off.

❋   ❋   ❋

A REWINDING THEN, THE morning unspooled, back through the crumbling arch, past the steam-blowing factories, the car dealerships, the fields of solar panels. Dust rose from scorched verges to fall in a fine mist upon the taxi windscreen. The road shimmered in the heat. In a field off the highway were the ruins of a third-century Roman settlement—she recalled her guidebook enthusing about the advanced and intricate nature of the drainage system. Plumbing, she thought, as they passed a field remarkable only for its scattered lumps of stone, a particularly historic piece of plumbing. "Stop here," she said to the driver, on spotting a signpost for a hiking trail. They were within sight of the Rifugio now, and she had no wish to field Allesandro's questions as to why she was back so early.

It was approaching noon and, as she walked, the heat was intense on her arms, her legs, the tops of her shoulders. Burrs and sap stuck to her skin, gathering seeds and petals. Inside the woods, the canopy of trees brought some relief. Here, the ground was dry as flint, crisp with pine needles that exuded a dry heat. It was like walking on a bed of matches, and she wouldn't have been surprised had they combusted beneath her feet. She arrived at a clearing where dozens of trees had been razed and the forest floor sloped to a cave mouth. A timber beam supported the entrance and into the timber two people called AL and RP had carved their initials, or perhaps one of them had carved their initials while the other looked on, indifferent. This place, too, she recognized from her guidebook. It was the cave where

villagers had hidden during the war and which had now become a shrine; she recalled an arty photo of candle stubs,
little coagulations of gray wax at the bottom of glass jars.

She squatted down and peered inside. The cave was not
entirely dark; narrow tunnels burrowed upward, creating
runnels of light. Squares of fabric cut from the clothes of the
sick, the dying, the already dead were fixed to the walls. She
should go in, she supposed; she should try to make the best
of this place that Sandra had landed her in, but instead she
settled herself on the ground beneath a tree. She shook pine
needles from her sandals, brushed the traces of the meadow
from her clothes. She leaned her head against the trunk and
closed her eyes. The humiliation of earlier had faded a little. It would return, of course, as humiliations always did; it
would wait for her in the long grass of memory. But for now
there was a restfulness to the light that filtered through the
trees, a tang, like incense, to the scent of pine needles.

She dozed a little. When she woke she found that the
sun had somehow pierced the barricade of leaves, and a
patch of skin on one arm was pinkening. She opened her
bag to get sunscreen and there it was: Etta's book, or, rather,
Etta's mother's book. Why on earth hadn't she left it behind
in Gariano? She turned it over in her hands, gingerly, as if it
might scald her, and knew immediately that she would never
again buy a book in that particular shade of blue, or any book
translated from the French, for that matter. There would be
no more Sacher torte or nutmeg, either. So many things ir-
revocably spoiled.

She got up and walked around to the other side of the tree, positioned the book upright against the trunk. But that was littering, wasn't it? She picked it up again. She could leave it in the cave, she supposed, next to all those grotty jars. She could pretend it was an offering of some sort, except some do-gooder might find it and attempt to repatriate it. She pictured pudgy do-gooder fingers punching out the phone number for Etta's mother. Walking a little distance from the cave, she scuffed at the ground with her sandals until she had a patch cleared of pine needles. A pointy stick looked like it might be of use. She poked the ground with it, but without much effect, and so she poked harder until it broke. She tried a stone then, which worked better. Dropping to her knees, she began to dig. When she encountered a root, she threw aside the stone and tugged, broke the root, flung it from her with a small yelp of triumph.

She continued digging with her hands until it occurred to her what she must look like: an animal crouched in the dirt, clawing. She stood up quickly and glanced about, as if someone might be watching her, laughing at her—*a whole new level of foolishness!*—but there were only trees, tall and inscrutable. Now that she'd stopped digging, there was utter silence apart from the back-and-forth of a bird on a branch above her head, the barely perceptible, flinted movements of its feet like the striking of tiny matches. She became aware of sweat running down her face. She placed the book in the hole—though it was not so much a hole as a small indentation—and heaped pine needles on top. It was a rather pathetic effort, she thought, when she stood back to observe it. No doubt come nightfall, a fox or other wild creature would come sniffing around; it would pick up her scent and, frenzied with hope, would dig in expectation of something bloody. She pictured the book dismembered, pages from spine, and scattered over the forest floor, its blue cover scored with the imprints of many small teeth.

She found a track that led back out to the meadow, but at a different point to where she'd entered earlier. There was a breeze and the grass rippled in a sea of dark greens, light greens, and silvers. She could see, a little distance away, the Rifugio and someone—Allesandro, she presumed—doing something with a ladder on the terrace. Farther uphill, half a dozen horses were grazing. The last film she and Sandra had seen together was set in medieval France, where horses kitted out for war—huge, apocalyptic horses in the king's colors—had galloped in a regal charge through cobbled streets, sweat glistening on their flanks. These horses were nothing like that. Most were not horses at all, but shaggy ponies. Possibly, one or two were donkeys.

Seemingly as one, they raised their heads from the grass and stared. The intent with which they regarded her was touching, as was the graveness with which they stood at attention, as if they had been waiting, as if her emergence from the woods had summoned them to a different, nobler, calling. She returned their gaze, keeping still, very still, even the in and out of her breathing as quiet as possible. Then she realized they were not looking at her, but past her. A figure was making his way up the hillside, a bucket in his hand. He came a little way up before halting and putting down the bucket. He cupped his hands around his mouth and began to call. The horses broke into a trot, then a canter. Then they were barreling downhill, their unkempt manes flying, their tails streaming out behind them. The slope brought its own momentum, and they were galloping now, neighing and snorting and whinnying. They thundered past, trampling on daisies, forget-me-nots, buttercups. And as they went by, she stepped back into the trees, to shelter from the clouds of yellow dust flung up by the chaos of their hooves.

SILHOUETTE

HER MOTHER'S ROOM WAS ON THE SECOND FLOOR WITH a view of the river and the Coca-Cola bottling factory on the opposite bank, neat rows of red-and-white trucks resembling from this distance a child's toy collection. Aileen had planned to deliver her news on Friday evening; that way, if things didn't go well, her mother would have time to come round before Aileen had to leave again on Sunday. But fog at Heathrow delayed her flight and then there was a queue at the rental car desk in Cork and a problem with a form, so it was almost eight P.M. before she arrived at the nursing home.

"Aileen," her mother said, "you're late." Her mother was propped up in bed, her slight frame barely denting the pillows. Settled by her bedside, in the room's only chair, was Eily, one of the other residents. Eily was tall as well as broad, her white curls adding several inches to her height, and when she leaned forward in the chair, she eclipsed Aileen's mother almost entirely.

"Sorry," Aileen said, "my flight was delayed." But her mother and Eily had already resumed their conversation. It was something about the new podiatrist and his tendency to be rough with the pumice stone. Her mother's problems, being terminal, were far beyond the reach of podiatry, but, still, she debated the subject of calluses with an intensity that was unsettling. Aileen went to stand by the window while she waited for them to finish. Their conversation had a curious dynamic—a decorous yet vaguely malicious chipping away at each other, the way a child might pick slyly at a scab. It occurred to her, fleetingly, that were she to deliver her news now, Eily's presence might possibly temper her mother's response. It wasn't that her mother had anything against grandchildren; but Aileen's sister, Janet, had already provided four, and the circumstances of Aileen's pregnancy—forty-three, unplanned, married work colleague—were not what her mother would have hoped for.

The nursing home had once been a convent, and it retained a cloistered feel. Cell-like rooms branched like pods off narrow stalks of corridors, and in the wall behind her mother's bed, there was a curious rectangular indent where it looked like a door had been papered over. Usually when she was home from London, she stayed in her mother's house in Ballyphehane, empty these days apart from a cat the neighbors had been entrusted with feeding. But Janet had rung earlier in the week to say that this time Aileen should book a hotel. There was now a tenant in their mother's house, because, as Janet had rather bluntly put it, it wasn't as if their mother would be moving back in. Aileen imagined a stranger, a girl—because for some reason she was sure the new tenant was a girl—working her way through the house, opening first one drawer, then another. "I guess this is what it feels like to be burgled," she'd said to Janet.

Janet had sighed. "It's nothing like being burgled," she said. "Why does everything have to be such a drama with you? I was only saying that to Mam the other night."

"So Mam knows?"

"About the house? Gracious, no! We were talking about something else."

"But what about my things?" Aileen had said. She'd pictured the girl—in clearer relief now: fair-haired and fine boned and dressed like a cat burglar—finding diaries from Aileen's teenage years, items of graying underwear forgotten in the airing cupboard.

"You haven't lived in that house in twenty years," Janet said. "What things could you possibly have there? If it makes you feel any better, I moved a lava lamp and a box of ornaments up to the attic."

It was late May, and the evening was still bright. Outside on the grounds, neatly pruned shrubberies descended into briars and mounds of fermented grass cuttings as they approached the river. Since Aileen's visit the previous month,

floods had taken away part of the boundary fence, and someone had bridged the gap with a length of blue rope, tied
between posts like a finish line. It was tempting fate, Aileen
thought; it was downright irresponsible in a place like this.
She imagined her mother and Eily, shuffling and elbowing,
as they tumbled downhill to land head over calloused heels
in the black mud of the riverbed.

Eventually, Eily stood up, gathering her dressing gown
around her, and shuffled toward the door. She paused to
raise a hand, hip height, in half salute, though her expression was so vexed the gesture could just as easily have been
interpreted as a threat. When Aileen sat in the vacated chair,
it still held traces of Eily's warmth, and she took off her coat
and folded it underneath her to serve as a cushion.

"I knew all the Reardons from Liscarroll," her mother
said, "and there was never any of them a dentist." A filigree
of bruises from the hospital drip was visible on the inside of
one arm. "There was a Reardon a vet, all right," she said. "A
vet of sorts, but never a dentist." This was her mother's latest
pastime: scrutinizing Eily's ancestry. Each new fragment was
committed to memory to be dissected in Eily's absence, in-
consistencies hunted down with a doggedness usually reserved for war criminals. Her mother's hand crept across the
blankets and beat up and down at the edge of the bed. "Janet
brought me a book the other night," she said. "You might as
well take it away." The book, a copy of *The Road*—a curious
choice for the terminally ill, Aileen thought—had fallen to
the floor, and Aileen picked it up, put it back on the locker.

"Take it with you when you're going," her mother repeated. "Things only go missing here," and she rolled her eyes in the direction of Eily's room.

From the corridor came the squeak of rubber-soled shoes and a trundling of wheels. A young woman in a blue aide's uniform parked a cart in the doorway. "How are we this evening?" she said, squeaking her way across the floor. She lifted Aileen's mother's hand and placed a finger on the underside of her wrist. The finger was plump and fat. Aileen's mother's skin was almost transparent, veins winding in blue rivers beneath the surface.

"Dorene," her mother said, "this is my other daughter, Aileen."

Dorene let go of her mother's hand and took a pen from the pocket of her uniform. She wrote something on the chart clipped to the bottom of the bed. "Daughter?" she said, as she peeled back the blanket and sheets on one side. "Why, you could be sisters."

Aileen felt offended, then immediately guilty, for was her mother not entitled to this at least, this small, transparent lie? She watched Dorene place a hand on her mother's back and roll her onto her side, as her other hand pulled taut the undersheet. There was something supremely confident in the way Dorene, who couldn't be more than thirty, moved her mother: easily, matter-of-factly, a careless squandering of touch as if this was something she did every day, which, of course, it was. Aileen suddenly felt very tired; tired and incompetent. If she could lift the baby out now she would. She would pass it, red and dripping, across the bed to Dorene. Dorene would know what to do with it. And Aileen knew then that she wouldn't be able to tell her mother about the baby this evening; she wouldn't be able to tell her anytime in this strange place that was half motel, half mortuary.

"I thought we might go for a drive tomorrow," she said, as soon as Dorene had gone. "Just you and me. I thought we might go to the seaside."

"I COULD ASK JANET to drive us," her mother said the next morning, as they stood on the porch of the nursing home. As she spoke, she patted the outcrop of silver curls at the nape of her neck, a nervous habit she'd had since Aileen was a child, though the curls had been brown then, and thicker.

"I know how to drive, Mam."

"It would be no trouble to Janet," her mother said, staring at the car parked beside the curb. "She could be here in twenty minutes." Aileen knew then that her mother had already asked Janet; that Aileen's driving—the likely hazards of it—had been debated in apocalyptic fashion until all her mother's troubles, even her illness, had paled beside the threat of a daughter home from London in a rented Fiat. Reminding herself that she mustn't fight with her mother, Aileen said nothing, just linked her mother's arm and walked her to the car.

They drove south along the coast with the sea on one side, and, on the other, ditches swollen with gorse and the lush, wanton grass of early summer. Last night, in a three-star hotel on the edge of the city, Aileen had taken out a map and decided they would go to Courtmacsherry, where her mother's family came from and where her mother had holidayed each summer when she was a child. Her mother was a poor passenger, flattening herself back against the seat every time they rounded a corner. Her hand flew to her throat if they overtook a lorry. Not a driver herself, she wasn't prepared to believe Aileen was one, either.

Janet texted to say she would meet them for coffee in Kinsale. Couldn't she have allowed her this one day alone with their mother? Aileen thought. But there was no safe way of saying this to Janet, no way that mightn't end in a row, so she'd said yes, of course, yes, please join us. Aileen and her mother were first to the café and sat at a table by the window. Aileen ordered coffee and a scone. Her mother ordered a pot of tea and a boiled egg, though boiled eggs weren't on the menu, then went to use the bathroom. Aileen thumbed through a copy of a local newspaper. She'd noticed a shift these past few weeks, her gaze falling on things previously skipped over, and now it settled on an article about hatches in Germany where women could leave their babies. She imagined something like the clothes-recycling unit outside her office. Babies tipping over into warm, scented heaps of other babies, downy and milky and sleeping; babies plopping into warm darkness, the occasional soft cracking of skulls like eggs.

From behind the bathroom door she heard the muffled

drone of the hand dryer, a drowsy, muted buzzing, like a bee trapped in a curtain fold. It stopped, started up again, stopped again. Her mother came out, wiping her hands on a paper tissue. "I don't know why they bother with those things," she said. She sounded more relaxed now, heartened perhaps by the fact that they had arrived unscathed. She took a plastic tub from her handbag and shook a blue cylindrical pill into her palm. Placing it on her tongue, she took a mouthful of tea and tipped back her head in a quick, jerky movement. She pressed a napkin to her lips, held it there a moment.

Janet's car pulled up outside. The eldest child, Keith, the one who looked most like Janet's husband, Richard, was in the passenger seat, the other three strapped into booster seats in the back. Janet took a while to parallel park, the minivan awkward and cumbersome, grazing the bumpers of the cars in front and behind. Then she swiveled round in the driver's seat, presumably, Aileen thought, to shout at the children, because she seemed to shout at them a lot. Instead, she produced from somewhere on the floor of the car a multipack of crisps and proceeded to distribute them. She got out of the car, locked it, and hurried up the steps of the café. "I couldn't get a babysitter," she said. "But we won't be long, will we?"

Now that Aileen saw her mother and sister together, there was a likeness—something in the nose, the chin—that she hadn't noticed before. The four children stared in from the car, eyes fixed on their mother, aunt, and grandmother. The older ones expertly ferried crisps to their mouths with small hands while the baby pulled at the teat of a bottle. Janet appeared to be expanding at the same rate that their mother was shrinking. Her sweater, one that Aileen had given her the Christmas before last, was at least two sizes too small. Janet settled herself in the chair beside her mother, directly opposite Aileen. "How are things in London?" she said.

"Pregnant," Aileen wanted to say. "Things in London are pregnant," but she didn't. She wondered how Janet would react when she, in turn, learned the news; pregnancy up to now had been Janet's territory. But Janet wasn't listening for her reply. She was looking out to the car where Keith was force-feeding crisps to the baby. "I'll crucify him," she said, and Aileen had an image of the boy nailed to the wall outside the café, blood dripping onto the flower boxes below. Janet jumped up and banged on the glass. "Stop it," she shouted. Inside the café, conversation ground to a halt, but outside, the children carried on regardless. Janet ran outside, tugged at the locked car door. She felt her pockets for the keys she'd left on the café table. "Open the door," she screamed.

Aileen's mother looked on with the detached air of a spectator at a bullring who was waiting for the main event to start. "She's got very fat," she said. "She didn't used to be that fat."

It was then that Aileen noticed the window above their

table was open. "She'd want to watch out," her mother said, "or Richard will look elsewhere. I always wondered about her marrying a younger man. I worried about it."

Aileen stood up and, too late, pulled the window shut. "He's only three years younger," she said.

Her mother seemed to take this as encouragement. "Well, yes, but three years is three years," she said, "And he's a man. Men are different." Their food had arrived and she took her boiled egg, began to strike it with a spoon all around the shell in sharp, brisk movements. Outside, the children had unlocked the door and now Janet was half in and half out of the car, walloping the children in turn, all of them except for the baby; walloping them with a force that made Aileen's hand go instinctively to her still-flat stomach.

Her mother took a mouthful of egg, then put the spoon down. "She used to be so pretty," she said. "She's let herself go." It was true, Aileen thought, looking at her sister. Janet used to be beautiful. "It's not easy to keep a man," her mother continued. "She'd want to be careful. Tidy herself up a bit." Aileen's father had died when she was three, so it wasn't as if their mother had had to worry too long about keeping him, but Aileen didn't say this. Janet slammed the car door and began to walk back toward the café entrance.

"It's the children, of course," Aileen's mother said. "Children do that to you."

Janet delayed for a while on the café porch. She appeared to be studying the posters on the notice board, advertisements for local fundraisers and sports fixtures and missing pets. When eventually she returned to the table, her eyes were red rimmed.

"You need to get Richard to have a word with that lad," her mother said, inclining her head toward the car where Crucifixion Keith was now crying in the passenger seat. "Otherwise he's only going to get worse. Best nip it in the bud."

Aileen imagined Janet putting their mother in a hatch and running away, their mother rolled up like a rug, her head tucked into her tummy, the soft, almost noiseless thud as she landed. And then, as if they'd been discussing something different entirely, as if Janet was not sniffling furtively beside her, their mother looked across the table at Aileen and said: "Remember those dolls you had when you were young?"

"Yes," Aileen said. It was hard to know where her mother might be going with this.

"I was only thinking about them the other day," her mother said. "You were still playing with them when you were twelve or thirteen. I used to worry about that. I thought maybe you were a bit slow."

"I collected dolls, Mam. Lots of girls did back then."

"Yes," her mother said. "Possibly you're right." And she nodded, but slowly, as if even now, thirty years on, she was still not fully convinced. "They very possibly did."

They said goodbye to Janet and the children and left the café, driving farther south until they reached Courtmacsherry and the sweep of the bay, the white fleck of waves, the boats rising and falling along the pier. There was a small public beach—a narrow strip of pebbly sand—and a hotel set back from the sea behind a line of rocks and a bank of low sand dunes. Access to the beach from the public parking lot was along a sloping path, and Aileen helped her mother out of the car and linked her arm as they made their way down together. Her mother moved slowly and with care, her eyes following the progress of her own feet over the sand. A dozen or more elderly women were gathered at the shore—hotel residents, Aileen presumed, because they all wore matching red swim caps. They were watching an instructor, a man young enough to be their grandson, demonstrate swim strokes. And then, as though a nudge from providence, a way into the conversation Aileen had determined she would have with her mother today, she saw in the water a pregnant woman. There was something loud, almost indecent, about her large belly, as if a hologram of her impregnation were stored beneath the skin. As she made her way in to shore, a strip of seaweed drifted across her path and she flung it away without breaking her stroke. How easy she made it look, Aileen thought, how effortless. She wouldn't have been surprised if the baby had swum out of her right then, without struggle, without pain, a small, shut-eyed thing carried in on the tide like a jellyfish. "She'd want to be careful," Aileen's mother said. "She's quite far along. I'd be worried about that."

"I'm sure she'll be fine," Aileen said. "She seems to be a strong swimmer."

"She's young, at least," her mother said. "She has that going for her. Too young, maybe. I doubt there's a husband."

They had reached a cluster of flat black rocks. Her mother's pace was slowing, her breath coming in ever-shorter gasps. Aileen looked at her and thought that she seemed to have shrunk since they left that morning. She wondered if the trip had been a mistake. But she'd asked the matron before setting out and the matron had said it should be fine, adding—rather curtly, Aileen thought—that she'd already told Janet the same thing. She helped her mother lower herself onto the flattest of the rocks to rest, and for a while they sat looking out at the sea and at the elderly women who were now moving farther out, yellow flotation devices tucked under their arms.

"I'm worried," her mother said.

Aileen waited. Over the years, her mother had so devalued the currency of worry that it was impossible to guess what might come next.

"About . . . you know," her mother said, "about what will happen."

"What will happen when?"

"You know . . ." her mother said. "What will happen at the end."

This was the first time her mother had addressed, directly, at least, the fact that she would soon die. "I'm afraid that there will be nobody there," she said.

Aileen thought they were about to embark on a spiritual discussion, but her mother said: "Not you, not Janet, not anybody." Her grip tightened on Aileen's hand. "There was a man from the ground floor died last week," she said. "Eily told me they couldn't find a vein in the end, and he was screeching for an hour before the ambulance arrived."

Aileen thought of the pregnancy chat rooms with their grotesque tales of forceps and episiotomies and thirty-hour labors. "Mam," she said, "don't be talking like that. You know I'll be there."

"You won't. You'll be in London."

"They'll contact me when . . ." Aileen wasn't sure when they would contact her. Because how, at this point, could they know, really know, from one minute to the next, when the end might be? "They'll contact me when the time comes," she said. "And anyway, Janet will be there."

"There's something wrong with Janet," her mother said. "I don't know what it is, but there's something wrong. I'm worried."

Aileen reached across and took her mother's hand. Farther up the coast, a kite surfer plowed a white furrow through the water. Aileen followed the plume of red and orange twisting in the sky above him as if the answer, the words she needed to next say to her mother, might be found up there. They sat in silence for a while. At the end of the day, Aileen thought, this was all she and her mother could offer one another, the comfort of being frightened together.

"I noticed you had a camera back in the car," her mother said. "I'd like you to take my photograph."

In the house in Ballyphehane, there had only ever been

two photos of her mother: one taken on her wedding day, the other some years earlier in a cousin's drawing room when her mother was still only a girl in a gingham dress and ankle socks, hair so fiercely parted it might have been done with a knife. "Yes, of course," Aileen said. "A photo would be lovely. I'll go get the camera." She looked at her mother. "Will you be okay here by yourself?"

"Certainly," her mother said. "Why wouldn't I be?"

The afternoon had turned cold and, as she walked, Aileen pulled her jacket tighter about her. She was passing through the dunes when a sudden dizziness struck, accompanied by the nausea that her doctor kept insisting was a good sign. She sat down for a moment, and, lying back on the grass, she closed her eyes. Here, by the seafront, the neat lawns of the hotel gave way to scrub colonized by clusters of yellow-eyed daisies and celandines. Back in London, the father of her child—how strange those words still sounded, "her child"—would be taking the younger of his two sons to a violin lesson. He'd accused her of being heartless, selfish, in her plan to have the baby. "The boys are six and ten," he'd said. "Have you considered at all what this will mean for them?" The nausea worsened and she tried to still her thoughts, to breathe slowly and deeply, but was foiled by the clamor of the gulls, circling and wheeling above the dunes. Their cries were sharp and high-pitched, almost human. As she lay there in the grass, they seemed to grow louder and shriller, and she sat up with a start, realizing that what she was hearing was not gulls, but women.

She ran back through the dunes to discover her mother in the sea, up to her waist in water. The hotel swimmers were making their way toward her, calling to her, their red bathing caps bobbing like stray buoys as they approached. Aileen ran down the beach, sliding and stumbling over the stones. She saw her mother tumble face forward and disappear for a couple of seconds beneath the surface. The instructor and one of the women had reached her now and were attempting to lift her, the water churning white in a mess of flailing arms and limbs. As Aileen waded out to meet them, they faced for shore and began to make their way back in, carrying her mother between them. They laid her down on the jetty wall and Aileen looked on as her mother coughed up water, spluttered, choked, coughed up some more, her hair plastered in wet strands to her skull.

They carried her mother to the hotel, up a long, straight avenue, with mature trees bordering the lawns on either side. Two peafowl, a hen and a cock, were foraging along the grass verge; they gently nudged and butted each other and raised their heads in lazy ambivalence as the party went by. Her mother was brought to a bedroom, and the hotel manager organized a robe and a pot of tea. One of the women offered a change of clothes—underwear and an oversized cardigan and skirt—which Aileen promised to return by post. Feeling nauseous again, she excused herself and went to the bathroom, where she vomited a little and splashed water on her face. She came out of the bathroom to hear her mother reciting her local pedigree to the other women as if she were a stud animal, delivering it in a singsong voice, like a poem learned at school. Aileen thought she could probably recite the list herself at this stage, she'd heard it often enough, though over the years her mother had become a little devious. Every so often, by way of erratum perhaps, or downright lie, she would slip in something hitherto unheard-of, some small, brazen embellishment.

When they were left alone, her mother ran a bath, refusing Aileen's offers of help. Every so often, Aileen knocked on the door to ask if she was all right, if she needed help washing her hair, but her mother said she didn't. "Call me when you want to get out," Aileen said through the door. She sat in a chair by the window and watched gulls stalk the lawn outside, and a group of children play tag on the beach, moving amphibiously between pools, cliff path, and rocks. After a while, she heard the gurgle of water down the plughole and pictured her mother attempting to clamber unaided from the bath, slipping on the wet floor. She went over to the bathroom, but when she put her hand to the door, she discovered it was locked.

Later that evening, back at the nursing home, Aileen got her mother into a nightdress and helped her into bed. At her mother's insistence, she went downstairs to the matron's office and fetched some brown paper to package up the borrowed clothes. "You'll send them tomorrow, won't you?" her mother said. "They'll only go missing here." Eily, mercifully, hadn't yet made an appearance this evening. Aileen topped up her mother's water glass. Beside the bed was a softly rounded groove in the floorboards. They were the original boards—eighteenth-century oak, according to the nursing home's brochure—and were peppered with small knotholes that spiraled away into blackness. Toward the end of the bed was another, identical, groove. A different bed must once have occupied this space, its ordinances closely but not exactly mirroring the one in which her mother now lay. Some other woman, perhaps a whole series of women, had lain here, night upon night, year upon year, mouths parted slightly in sleep, all the time pressing this memento of their existence into the timber.

Her mother took a sip of water, then lay back on the pillows, closing her lips tightly against the offer of more. "You forgot to take that book last night," she said. "Don't forget it this time. There's nothing safe here." And as Aileen picked up the book and put it in her bag, it occurred to her that these might very well be her mother's last words.

On the way back to her hotel, she took the slip road for Ballyphehane. Her mother's house was a modest two-bedroom townhouse in a not-so-fashionable area, and she wondered now how Janet had managed to find a tenant for it. She parked directly outside. She would be polite, she told herself; calm and polite. The tenant—the girl—would understand; Aileen would understand if it were her. She would say that she knew it was the girl's home now, that she, Aileen, only wanted a look around, that she had come all this way. As she sat in the car, she rehearsed two speeches: one for if the girl turned out to be pleasant, the other for if she was rude. All the time she was rehearsing, she saw the girl as clearly as if she were standing in front of her, still fine boned and blond, still dressed like a cat burglar.

She was about to step out of the car when she noticed that the front garden was straggling and uncared for, her mother's precious lupines listing sideways and choked by weeds. She experienced a sudden burst of anger toward the girl, who she decided now would most likely be rude. To one side of the front door an overflowing trash bin was disgorging its contents onto the path. The curtains were missing from the living room window—she could imagine what her mother would say about that—and she could see beer cans on the coffee table and the silhouette of someone on the couch watching television. But the silhouette was not of a girl, fine boned or otherwise. It was that of a man and when, perhaps having noticed the car, he stood up and came to the window, she saw that it was Janet's husband, Richard. The garden was small, no more than half a dozen yards from porch to gate, and she knew he must have recognized her. She waited, wondering if he might go to the door and invite her in, but he remained at the window, and after a moment she turned the key in the ignition and drove away.

At the end of the street she went east, skirting the edges of the city as she made her way back to her hotel. Tomorrow she would say goodbye to her mother at the nursing home and would catch her flight back to London. The nausea that usually renewed its onslaught at this hour was missing this evening; her doctor had told her it would go in time, that she shouldn't worry when it did. She found that in its absence, without its bittersweet niggling, she felt nothing, no sense of anything beyond herself, and so she tried to summon an image. All that offered itself was a grainy composite of other women's scans, a shadowy thing floating in a sea of amniotic fluid. For a moment, as she waited at traffic lights, it took on features, morphed into a girl, fair-haired and fine boned. Its eyes were tightly shut, the way her mother's eyes had been when she came out of the water that day, steeled against the sting of salt. Her mother, who, it had seemed to Aileen, had been striking out with the last of her strength, her arms raised in resistance against her rescuers, her face set to open sea.

A DIFFERENT COUNTRY

———

AT KINNEGO THE LIGHT WAS SILVER, THE SEA AND SKY gray, and the wind that snatched at her breath had a sharp, almost metallic, edge. Anytime he had spoken of this place he had always spoken of the light and now, early morning, the beach deserted, she understood what he meant. They had traveled from Dublin the day before but had left late, then stopped too long in Derry, so that it was dusk before they drove north along the Foyle. The sea was already slipping into darkness then, the cabin lights of a boat carried like a lamp up the estuary, and as they passed through Quigley's Point, Moville, Greencastle, small dark shapes cut the air above the water: birds, perhaps, or bats from the trees that grew along the shore road.

※ ※ ※

WAKING THAT MORNING IN his brother's bungalow, she had pulled back the bedroom curtains to get a proper look at the sea and had found herself staring at a concrete wall, roughly plastered, set no more than three or four feet back from the house. Beneath the window, filling the space between it and the wall, was a tangle of orange netting, half a dozen crudely cut lengths of galvanized sheeting, and a stack of plastic boxes stamped with the logo of a fisherman's co-op.

"It's a boat shed," Jonathan said from the bed, and she had turned to see him raised on one elbow, watching her in amusement.

"But why here?" she said, gesturing in disbelief to the wall. "Why block out the sea, the light?" It was cold in the bedroom, her breath misting the glass as she leaned closer to the window. The net held remnants of the sea: strips of black, leathery seaweed, thin as bootlaces, and a handful of barnacles. "Imagine," she said, conscious of his eyes on her as she shivered in her nightdress, "what a view like that would be worth in Howth."

He had laughed, patting the pillow next to him. "You're not in Kansas now, Dorothy," he said, and as she climbed back under the blankets he put his hand on the jut of her hip and pulled her close.

They drove to Kinnego first thing after breakfast, before anyone else was up. They parked at the top of a rocky headland, and as she stepped out of the car the wind almost pulled the door from her grasp. Below them the bay lay wide and empty, the cliffside a tangle of green, bushy vegetation sloping to the water. She held his hand as they descended the steep path to the beach. "A ship from the Spanish Armada was wrecked here," he said, putting an arm around her waist to steady her. "An old Venetian trading ship, converted for battle."

She stopped and tucked her hair down the back of her jacket to keep it from blowing about her face. "Did many people drown?"

He nodded. "Aye, and the locals ate the ones that didn't. Or so we were told as children."

"That's a myth, obviously," she said.

"Wait until you've met the locals."

"You're a local," she said, but already he had dislodged her from the crook of his arm and was striding ahead of her across the sand, over to the tidal pools where rocks, black and sleek, broke the surface of the water.

A dog was loose on the beach, a long-haired black-and-white creature, and now it came tearing across the sand toward her, its ears flat to its head, its tail swinging like a rudder. It skidded to a halt in front of her and, opening its mouth, dropped something at her feet. "What's that you've got for me?" she said.

It was a crab, the shell a buttermilk color with a sprinkling of green, like mildew, and a darker green along its scalloped rim. It wriggled as she held it between thumb and forefinger, its grayish legs slow and jerky, like the legs of the old men in bathing trunks at the Forty Foot on Christmas mornings. She tapped the shell and the crab stopped wriggling, drew its legs up into its belly.

The dog leaped in the air, snapping at the crab. "Now I get it," she said. "You want me to throw it." The dog whined, skittered back and forth on the sand. "That wouldn't be very nice, would it?" she said. She held the crab above her head with one hand, ruffling the dog's ears with the other. The dog barked. "You don't understand, do you?" she said. She walked to the edge of the waves and, bending down, released the crab into the water.

The dog yelped and tore into the spray. When the crab was carried back in on the next wave, he seized it and dropped it again at her feet. "No!" she said, snatching it up. "Bad dog!" The shell was slimy with dog slobber and a crack had appeared, running top to bottom. This time she took a couple of steps into the sea, her new suede boots wet to above the ankle, ice-cold water seeping through to her socks. She flung the crab as far as she could in a high, curved arc and once more the dog charged after it.

She was coming out of the waves, her boots heavy with water—ruined, she thought, the salt would ruin them, they would never be the same—when she saw Jonathan walking toward her, his shoulders hunched against the wind. His stride was long and easy, and he had his hands in his pockets, his hair blown back from his forehead. He reached her just as the dog emerged from the sea, dripping and victorious, and deposited the crab at his feet.

"What's this?" he said. "Some sort of Dublin pastime? We mostly use sticks here."

He tried to kiss her but she pushed him away and bent to pick up the crab. The dog retched a couple of times, then coughed up something small and gray, and she saw that it was a crab leg. "Scram!" she said to the dog, and she stamped her foot. "Shoo! Go home!" but the dog just barked and hurled himself at her, almost knocking her over. The crab was split open, pearly white flesh visible where the shell was lifting away from the body. Two legs were missing, another hanging from a sliver of tissue.

She handed the crab to Jonathan. "You throw it," she said. "It needs to go farther out."

He inspected the crab as it lay motionless on his palm. He poked it with his finger but still it didn't move. "I'm afraid it no longer has any needs," he said. He tossed it over his shoulder, where it shattered against some rocks, and the dog was away like a rocket, snuffling around in shallow pools after bits of shell, pieces of leg.

THE TIRES SPUN ON wet grass as she reversed the car onto the road, and they headed back toward Greencastle, past the lighthouse and the lighthouse keeper's cottage, past an old schoolhouse, converted now, hanging baskets straggling with last summer's flowers. Looking down at the beach, she glimpsed a streak of black and white: the dog darting back and forth along the water's edge. Though it was autumn, the

cliffside was still green, fuchsia bright in the ditches, heath-
ers blooming rust and orange in the bogs beyond. It was
almost too beautiful, she thought, the colors too pure, the
light too fantastical. It was as if she were driving through the
landscape of a computer game, the steering wheel her con-
sole, and the walls of the too-white cottages might crumble
as she passed, revealing dark, monstrous creatures with the
gristle of Spanish sailors between their teeth. She glanced at
Jonathan in the passenger seat beside her and for a moment
she did not know him, and Dublin, her home, the university,
all seemed very far away.

His brother's bungalow stood with its back to the sea in
a sloping field of briars and reeds accessed by a narrow side
lane. There must once have been a gate, but only a pair of
hinges, thick with rust, remained, set into wooden posts on
either side of the entrance.

"I'd knock it all down," he'd said, when they arrived the
night before, "all," as far as she could see, being the bungalow, a concrete shed with a domed roof that turned out
to be the boat shed, and a wooden coal bunker. "I'd level it
and start again, take it closer to the water." Everywhere they
went, this was what he did, and she had come to understand
that he couldn't help himself. He was an architect, one year
out of university, where they had met in his final term. He
saw derelict outhouses and boarded-up petrol stations and,
almost instinctively, ghosted up their future, measured it out
in his head in steel and wood and light.

Outside the back door, a blue Fiat without tires or windscreen was raised on a platform of concrete blocks. Its roof was covered in a mulch of dead leaves and rust dappled the paint. It's the salt that does that, she thought, pleased that she understood. It's the salt that causes the rust, because how often in Howth had she listened to her father complain about the very same thing, although the rust on her father's car was never as deep an orange, never as widespread.

Pauline, his brother's girlfriend, had been in bed when they left the house that morning. Now she was at the stove, frying an egg in a blackened pan. She was heavily pregnant, one hand resting on the small of her back, the other shaking the pan, sliding the egg back and forth. "Come in quick," she said, "and close that door. It's wild cold today." She tipped the egg onto a plate, where it quivered in a pool of grease, and then she filled the kettle at the sink.

She was good-looking in a raw, violent sort of way: black hair loose about her shoulders; thick, unplucked brows. She wore a checked shirt and tracksuit bottoms and, although it was late October, a pair of flip-flops. Her toenails were crudely cut, the skin of her heels hard and yellow. She reminded Sarah of the girls from the estates in Castlebar when she went to visit her cousins in the summer: girls in the backyards of pubs after closing time, resting half-finished pints on empty kegs; girls propped against alley walls, taking boys like bullets.

There was a table in the center of the kitchen covered with a square of blue-checked oilcloth that barely reached the edges. A potted plant, dense and woody, with dark-green variegated leaves sat on a lace doily. Pauline lowered herself into a chair and began to eat her egg. Her shirt was too small, and when she reached for the salt it rose to reveal a dark line, like a dorsal stripe, running from her belly button into the waistband of her tracksuit. "Your brother's away to Killybegs with the van," she said. "He'll be back later." She patted her stomach. "I hope the wee babby doesn't take a notion to come early." As she spoke, her stomach shifted of its own accord, broke into a furious bulging and rippling.

Sarah sat beside her and slipped off her wet boots. Jonathan was making tea, taking mugs from the draining board, a box of Sainsbury's tea bags from a shelf in the corner. Whatever the bungalow's architectural failings, he was at ease inside it, opening cabinet doors, rooting about to find sugar and biscuits. "The baby won't come early," he said. "And anyway, if it does, I'm here."

When Pauline laughed, her front teeth were white but slightly crooked, one edging in front of the other, the way Sarah's had done before she got braces. "Towels and hot water, is it, Johnny? No offense, but I'd have it in the field first."

"I meant," he said, joining them at the table, "that we'd drive you to the hospital."

He went to pour Pauline's tea, but she waved him away. "Wild bad heartburn from the tea," she said.

A window looked out on the narrow lane to the side of the bungalow, while another overlooked the rough ground toward the back. Though it was barely noon, the sky had darkened and a bank of cloud was forming above the estuary. A clothesline ran from a hook on the boat shed wall to a pole in the field, and the wind tore at a pair of blue overalls, whipping them into a frenzy, arms and legs flailing. Sarah unbuttoned her coat and hung it on the back of her chair, and, as she did, the scarf around her neck slipped to the floor.

Pauline noticed it first. She picked it up but instead of returning it, held on to it, rubbing the fabric back and forth between her fingers, stroking it. "Burberry?" she said, inspecting the label, and she raised her dark eyebrows.

Sarah felt herself blush. "Jonathan gave it to me," she said, "for my birthday."

"Jonathan?" Pauline said, looking at him across the table, and she laughed. "Well, Jonathan, your taste has improved. They must have taught you something down in Dublin." She slapped him playfully in the face with the scarf and laughed again, more softly this time. "Very nice, Jonathan," she said, repeating the name as if it were a joke. "Nice, but wild, dear," and she put the scarf down on the table.

Sarah drank her tea and listened to Jonathan and Pauline talk about people she didn't know, people with strange, improbable names such as Jimmy High Boy, Larry the Wren, Frank the Post. She heard Jonathan's accent shift little by little to match Pauline's, until it became something different, something foreign. And, as she listened, it seemed to her that the border they had crossed and uncrossed the night before, the black line cutting through villages and sitting rooms, was little more than artifice, a nod to some sem-

blance of containment. It was a belt slung loosely, land and
sea spilling over it like paunch, because here, here, too, it
was a different country.

A white HiAce van drove up the lane, trailing exhaust
fumes, and turned in at the bungalow. It parked next to
the blue Fiat, and a man, tall and thin, got out. They had
not met the night before, but she knew it was Jonathan's
brother as soon as he walked by the window. He had the
same high cheekbones, though his were veined and ruddy,
and he walked with the same long stride. He paused on the
doorstep to take off his boots. "All right, Johnny?" he said,
and he winked. "State visit, is it?" He was in his early thirties,
hair so tightly shaved it was barely a shadow on his skull, fair
eyebrows disappearing into his face. He crossed the kitchen
in his socks and slapped Jonathan on the back. He held out
a hand to Sarah. "I'm Aidan," he said.

Under his arm was a parcel wrapped in plastic and secured with blue twine. He placed it on the table and began
to untie it, his hands red and scarred, one finger ending in
a round, pink stub just above the knuckle. When he peeled
back the plastic, a pile of fish spilled out. He picked one up,
a black, monstrous thing over a foot and a half long, car-
toonish in its ugliness: a wide mouth studded with teeth;
white, wiry filaments protruding from its forehead. Pauline
reached for it, sliding her fingers through the red flap of its
gill. "There's a beauty," she said, and she nodded at Sarah. "I
bet you haven't seen one of these in Dublin."

"She hasn't seen one here, either," Aidan said, and they all laughed, everyone except Sarah.

"Och, what harm a few fish?" Pauline said. "Pure sinful to throw them back and half the world starving."

Aidan parceled up the fish again, tossing them one on top of another in a black, slippery mound, and put them in the fridge. He took out a packet of cigarettes and offered one first to Sarah. When she refused, he lit one for Pauline and another for himself.

Pauline settled back in her chair, her hands resting on the dome of her belly, smoke from the cigarette curling toward the ceiling. "Your uncle Seamus rang this morning. He says he'll leave the wee outboard tied up at the pier in Moville."

"Aye," Aidan said, taking a pull of his cigarette. "That'll do rightly." He didn't join the others at the table, but remained standing, leaning against the kitchen wall.

Pauline blew smoke out the corner of her mouth. "You're not taking a wee boat like that out tonight, surely?"

"I'm not going far, just off the shore in Shroove."

"Is Seamus going with you?"

"I'm going on my own."

Pauline tapped ash into her empty plate. "What sort of a job is it, anyway?"

Aidan put a hand to the back of his neck, kneaded the skin as if soothing a sore muscle. "Trouble with the nets," he said.

Pauline stared at him. She said nothing for a moment,

and then she looked away. She reached past Sarah and picked up a copy of the *Derry Journal* that lay at the end of the table. "That's not a job for this kind of weather," she said, opening the newspaper.

"It's not a job for any kind of weather. It might as well be tonight."

Pauline shook her head. "Only a fool would be out by himself in a wee boat tonight." There was silence in the kitchen apart from the crackle of the newspaper as she turned the pages.

Sarah became conscious of the in and out of her own breath, the soft drumming of someone's foot, perhaps her own, on the kitchen tiles. She thought of gathering up the mugs and taking them to the sink to wash them, but before she could do anything, she heard Jonathan say to his brother, "I'll go with you."

Aidan's hand left the back of his neck and began to caress the bony contours of his skull. "You're maybe accustomed to a different kind of boat these days, Johnny," he said. "It's not a yacht, now," but this time, nobody laughed.

"I sailed the half-decker to Tory the summer our father died," Jonathan said. "And I sailed it to Rathmullan the time of the oyster festival the summer after."

All of the years he had lived in this place before he met her, all of the time they had been strangers to each other, unaware of the other's existence, settled upon Sarah, heavy and impenetrable. She felt a small, quiet panic rise up inside of her. It was the panic of a swimmer who has drifted out, little by little, on a rogue current and who suddenly discovers herself to be far from shore. She had a sense of something slipping away from her; it was something she could not quite identify, but she could feel its ebbing nonetheless.

"That was a long time ago," Aidan said. "You haven't been out since. Likely you've forgotten, and maybe you're better off."

"You know rightly there's no forgetting." Pauline stubbed out her cigarette and stood up. Her belly swung low and heavy as she walked across the kitchen to the airing cupboard and switched on the water heater. "I'm not feeling well," she said. "I'm going to take a shower and then I'm going back to bed, and you boys can go to Shroove or to any damn place you like."

As Pauline left the kitchen, Sarah had a sudden image of her naked: the distended belly, the hair, black and wet and sleek, writhing in worms around her shoulders. She saw her in the small, dark bathroom in the shadow of the boat shed, standing under the shower as the water sluiced over her, a sea creature lured to dry land.

OUT ON THE ESTUARY, a trawler had dropped anchor for the night, light from the engine room pooling on the water. As Sarah drove along the narrow coast road, she saw matchstick figures moving about the floodlit deck. Beside her, Pauline emerged from the grip of a contraction and sank back in the passenger seat. She pushed her hair, damp with sweat, from her face and took out her phone. "I'll try him again," she said. They were a mile beyond Greencastle, past the fishery school and the holiday homes clustered in the shadow of the fort, heading toward Shroove.

On the other side of the estuary, a string of evenly spaced lights, brighter than street lights, ran along the edge of the peninsula. Sarah had asked Jonathan about them the night before as they took their luggage from the boot of the car. "Is that a hotel?" she said, and he had laughed, shaking his head as he walked toward the back door. "That's Magilligan Prison," he said. Later, he told her how as a child he had gone there with his father to visit a cousin. "What was it like?" she said, but he had been unable to remember much, only some Nissen huts from the war and a soldier walking four or five dogs on a chain. The prison glittered now across the water, its perimeter lights threaded like a string of bright beads along the ragged coastline.

Pauline swore as Aidan's phone clicked once more into voicemail. "Likely they're still at that job," she said, "and if they are, they'll not hear a phone. Or if they hear it, they'll not answer." She reached for the holdall at her feet and hauled it onto her belly, rooting through nightdresses and slippers until she found her cigarettes. "Try Jonathan," Sarah said and she began to call out the number, but Pauline cut her short. "I already have," she said. She lit a cigarette and rolled down the car window to let the smoke out.

Her hair appeared blacker than usual against the pallor of her skin, her dark brows like slashes of war paint. "My daddy's a fisherman," she said. "My granddaddy, too, same as Aidan's." She touched a hand lightly to her stomach. "And there's days I'm standing at the end of the pier and I could swear that this wee babby knows. I can feel him straining for the sea, the same as if he could see it or smell it." She took a drag of her cigarette, blew out a mouthful of smoke. "But it's a dirty business, fishing. Dirty and hard. You're lucky, with Johnny." She tossed the cigarette out the window and clutched her stomach. "Here comes another one," she said, and she doubled over, resting her forehead on the dash.

Coming out of the boglands, they were forced into the ditch by a small car that careered toward them in a blaze of headlights. It bounced off the road, temporarily airborne, then sped away, a boy in a dark hoodie sunk low in the driver's seat. "One of the Shaker Sweeneys from the Malin Road," Pauline said, and Sarah waited for her to say more, but she leaned back and closed her eyes. In the rearview mirror, the taillights of the receding car flickered red and were gone, extinguished, the road returned to darkness.

Pauline didn't speak again until they passed the sign for Shroove. A pub rose out of the blackness, an oasis of light on the otherwise desolate stretch of coast. "I had my debs there," she said. "Four years ago last summer."

Sarah had thought of Pauline as older—not older in the way that her parents were older, but older certainly than herself and Jonathan. Now she realized they were practically the same age. "Did you take Aidan?" she said. She tried to imagine Aidan in a tuxedo, a grown man awkward in a room full of teenagers, his hands red and calloused below the white cuffs of a dress shirt.

"I didn't know Aidan then," Pauline said. "I took Johnny. Johnny and I were at school together in Carn," and as the lights of the pub fell away behind them, she said, "Here! Turn in here," and she pointed to a gap in a field.

The grass was littered with cans and the charred circles of spent fires. The field ran to a line of low cliffs, with the sea, dark and choppy, stretched out beyond. Sarah stopped the car. Pauline was bent over, moaning, and when she lifted her face from her hands there were tears running down her cheeks. "They'll be down at the shore," she said. "Tell him to hurry."

Sarah found a flashlight in the boot and followed a trail through the grass to the edge of the cliff. Below her, she saw lights bobbing on the water and, when her eyes adjusted to the darkness, the outline of a boat. There was a secluded beach: a strip of white sand, stark against the black of the surrounding rocks. The sea was silvered by the moon and by the lights of Magilligan across the estuary, and as she watched the boat cut ripples through the water she was struck by how very beautiful it all was, beautiful and unspoiled, and how, if it were not for Pauline waiting in the car, she would have liked to stay.

She began to descend the steep path to the cove, clutching at reeds to steady herself. The slope propelled her forward so that she was unable to stop even if she wanted to, and in the end she half-ran, half-fell onto the small beach.

The cove was quiet, apart from the slap and fizz of waves breaking on the sand. The men had cut the boat's engine and Jonathan jumped overboard, began to wade toward her. He was wearing a dark-colored oilskin, the hood pulled tight around his face. "What are you doing here?" he said when he reached her, and she realized that it was not Jonathan, but Aidan. He had something long, like a stick, tucked under his arm.

"Where's Pauline?" he said when she did not answer, but she was transfixed by a shape twisting out beyond him on the water, something thrashing and struggling, the sea churning white all around. She thought with sudden fright that it was a body, but then she saw that there were many of them, and they were moving slowly inland, plowing furrows through the dark sea. They looked like divers in wetsuits, but as they got closer, she saw that they were seals, black and lustrous. They were rolling in on the waves, disappearing below the water, then surfacing again, moonlight glinting on their sleek heads.

"Where is she?" Aidan said again. He caught Sarah by the shoulder and shook her, and she realized that the thing under his arm was not a stick, but a gun.

"She's in the car," she said. "The baby's coming." She jumped back as a wave rushed in, wetting her shoes and the ends of her jeans.

The boat was close to shore now, Jonathan standing at the helm. Another wave rolled in and a seal came crashing onto the beach. It landed with a thud on its back then flipped over onto its stomach. It lay bleeding on the sand by Sarah's feet and when she dropped to her knees, she saw the hole in the side of its head where it had been shot. "Oh my God," she said, letting the flashlight fall from her hand. "Oh my God, oh my God."

"Give me the car keys." Aidan was standing over her, his hand outstretched.

"They're in the ignition," she said, without looking at him, and he turned and broke into a run, back up the cliff path, the gun still under his arm.

The boat was within a few meters of shore and Jonathan stepped out, pulled it up onto a bank of pebbles. He, too, wore an oilskin, the hood tight around his face, and waders that reached to the top of his thighs. "They've got brazen," he said, walking toward her across the sand. "They've been eating through the nets, destroying the catch." He held out a hand to help her up, but she didn't take it.

A wave thundered in and, farther up the cove, another seal was tossed onto the beach. She left the first seal and ran to the second. This one was smaller—a pup, she thought— its skin a lighter color. Blood dribbled from its mouth and from a wound in its neck, and all along the edges of the rocks the tide foam was stained a deep pink.

Jonathan had followed, slowly, across the sand, and now he stood looking down at her, his hands in his pockets. "Is Pauline okay?" he said. "Is it the baby?"

Sarah was crouched beside the seal. It was still alive, a

steady trickle of blood coming from its mouth, its chest rising and falling.

"We'll take the boat back to Moville," Jonathan said. "The van's parked at the pier. You'll need to change before we go to the hospital."

She rubbed at her wet jeans, tried to brush away the pebbles and bits of broken shell that clung to them, and saw that they were stained with the seal's blood. And still the waves charged in, an incessant advance and retreat, and, a few feet away, the body of another seal somersaulted onto the rocks. "We can't leave them like this," she said. She reached out a hand and touched the seal pup's head. It flinched but did not pull away, its eyes, black as onyx, beginning to lose focus.

"They're almost dead," he said, and she could hear the impatience in his voice. "The tide will carry them back out." He was already walking away from her, toward the boat. "Come on," he said, as he dragged it to the water. "Climb in."

She got to her feet and looked around the beach. The wind had eased, the night sky was clear, and the clean, white bones of a dead seabird were scattered across the sand like pieces of carved ivory. At the base of the cliffs, a length of timber, slime green and rotting, was jammed between two rocks. She dislodged it and dragged it back across the sand to where the seal lay dying.

Jonathan shouted to her from the water. "What are you doing?" he said. To the south, beyond the village, lights appeared on the cliff top, the headlights of a car pulled in on the coast road. "Come on," he said. "We need to get out of here," and he jumped into the boat.

She stood over the seal and raised the piece of timber. She heard the splutter of an engine and saw Jonathan standing in the boat, waiting for her. He did not speak or call and he appeared only in silhouette, his face featureless under the dark oilskin. She looked down at the seal and saw its half-closed eyelid flicker. All around her, the shore glittered like a sequined cloth, tiny shells and pebbles luminous in the moonlight, even as blood darkened the sand. She stood there, the timber held high above her head, the seal bleeding out at her feet. And all the time the waves rushed in, remorseless, and, beautiful across the water, steadfast and unblinking, shone the lights of Magilligan.

THE SMELL OF DEAD FLOWERS

———

THE HOUSE ON DRUMCONDRA ROAD WAS A DOUBLE-
fronted red-brick with bay windows and a wooden door set
back into an arched porch. I put down my suitcase and rang
the bell. A huddle of sickly plants, brittle stemmed and arid,
stood in pots on the front step. There was an elaborate twisting of keys in locks, a sliding across of bolts, and all the time
Lou Anne shouting at me to "hold on," as if, after making the
journey from Tuamgraney, I might turn around and go back
again. "How was the bus?" she said when finally I stepped
inside, and then, without waiting for my reply, "How was the
taxi?"

Lou Anne was my mother's cousin, and her house was
on the bus route to the university. She was the same age as
my mother, somewhere in her early forties, but her clothes
were unlike anything my mother might wear: a knee-length

turquoise dress, gold braiding at the collar and sleeves, an amber brooch squatting like a beetle on her shoulder. Her hair was henna red, tied in a ponytail with the faintest tide-mark of gray around the temples. She had her back to me and was busy with the door, bolts squealing like pigs as she coaxed them into place. On the hall stand was a telephone, something we hadn't yet got at home. There was a rug that didn't quite stretch the full width of the hall, so that along the edges I caught a glimpse of black-and-white checkered tiles. Several leaves lay scattered about, carried in perhaps by the wind because above the door a small square of glass was missing from the fanlight.

Finished at last with the bolts, Lou Anne turned to me. "Look at you," she said. "All grown up," and she shook her head, as if my reaching adulthood were something she hadn't countenanced. She reached for my hand but didn't shake it. Instead she straightened out my fingers, and worked her way from one to the next, pinching the middle joints. "You have good hands," she said. Her own hands were bumpy and stubby fingered, not at all how I imagined the hands of a pianist, but then it was only ever my mother who called her that; my father called her "the hippie" or "the head case," sometimes "the communist," depending on his mood, and on how he was getting along with my mother. Because in the way that Lou Anne was my mother's cousin and not my father's, so, too, was she my mother's friend.

I unzipped my shoulder bag and brought out the box of perfumed soaps my mother had gift-wrapped, purple ovals inlaid with flower petals. "There was no need for anything like that," Lou Anne said, but already she was tearing open the wrapping paper. I looked at her—her legs bare under the gold-braided dress—and thought my mother had got it wrong, Lou Anne was not a gift soap sort of woman, but she pried an oval from its plastic hollow and pinched it the way she had pinched my fingers. She seemed genuinely pleased. "Lavender," she said, bringing it to her nose and sniffing. "Your mother and I went through a phase when we would wash ourselves with nothing else." She pressed the oval back into its plastic nest and dislodged a little half-moon of soap from under her nail. She smiled at me then, and I saw that she was quite beautiful and younger looking, when she smiled, than my mother.

Somewhere upstairs a door opened, and a young woman appeared on the landing. She was tall and plump, her round-ness apparent even from this distance beneath blue paja-mas. The last time I'd met Cassie, we'd both been children, and I was startled to see her now, in body at least, a grown woman. "You remember my daughter," Lou Anne said, and I had a sudden, vivid recollection of a day at our farm when I was ten and Cassie twelve, when she'd squatted to pee outside the milking parlor, sending a yellow stream winding through the dust of our yard. The exact nature of Cassie's disability was never discussed in our house. She rarely spoke and was sickly, as well as being what my father called "back-ward," though my mother would tut-tut whenever he used that word. Cassie still wore her hair in two dark brown plaits, at odds now with her new adult shape. Lou Anne called up the stairs. "Go back to your room," she said. "I'll be up in a while," and Cassie turned, retreated across the landing. "Come on," Lou Anne said then, putting the box of soaps down on the hall table, "I'll show you your bedroom."

The hall had been clean enough, well-kept apart from the unmended fanlight and a lingering smell of cooking, something spiced and unidentifiable. Climbing the stairs behind Lou Anne, I saw a layer of dust along the dado rail and on the picture frames. Four doors led off the landing. One was partly open, and I could see the enamel corner of a bath, and blue and white tiles on the wall. "I've put you in Daddy's old bedroom," Lou Anne said, pushing open a door. "It's Daddy's old bed, the springs are a bit rickety, but the mattress is new." The air felt older here than in the hall, thicker, as if it had been fermenting. Lou Anne went over to the window and opened the curtains to let some light in. "We haven't used this room in a while," she said. "I did try to sleep here once after Daddy died, but it was just too strange." There was a bed beneath the window, and at the foot of the bed a wardrobe. Shoehorned into one corner was a desk in cheap plywood, the self-assembly kind, newer than the rest of the room, with a lamp and a vase of yellow flowers that looked suspiciously like dandelions. "Marcus made the desk," Lou Anne said. "We had to take off the skirting board to get it to fit." Marcus. My mother had mentioned another lodger; he was "from the country, too," which seemed to give her some comfort, though I knew she'd be better comforted were he a girl. "I'll leave you to it," Lou Anne said. "Come downstairs when you've unpacked and we'll have a bit of supper."

As I hung up my clothes, I could hear Cassie moving about in the next room, the occasional creak of bedsprings, the soft thud of things dropped. I wondered if Marcus was home, and listened out for other sounds, but there were none. In the wardrobe I found a plastic bag full of men's ties, paisley patterned with the knots hardened into them. They still held the smell of Lou Anne's father, a smell of sweat and tobacco, and I pushed the bag to the very back and stood my empty suitcase on top of it. When everything was put away, I sat on the edge of the bed and watched, through the net curtains, traffic going by on the road outside. I sat there for as long as I thought I could get away with and, when I could put it off no longer, I went downstairs.

I found Lou Anne in a room toward the front of the house setting a circular table with cutlery. "Can I help with anything?" I said, because my mother had warned me a hundred times that I must offer to help.

"It's just a bit of cold meat and salad," she said. "I have it ready in the fridge."

This room had a wounded look, a sense of damage inflicted from myriad tiny skirmishes over many years. It was heavy with furniture: As well as the dining table and chairs there was a tallboy with dusty cacti; a nest of tables piled with out-of-date telephone directories; glass-fronted cupboards crammed with yellowing silverware. I imagined what my father would say if he saw it, how he would delight in its chaos, squirreling away details to use as ammunition against my mother. Against one wall was a piano strewn with magazines and other paraphernalia, so that it looked like some effort would be required to raise the lid.

Lou Anne returned with plates on a tray: slices of yellow-crumbed ham beside circles of almost translucent cucumber and quartered tomatoes, spoonfuls of different kinds of salad. This was what my mother served to visitors, though Lou Anne's version was less practiced: Already the pickled beetroot was bleeding red juices into the coleslaw, turning it pink. "Sit, sit," she said, and as I took a seat I noticed that there were four place settings. Lou Anne was busy now with a tea set, cups and saucers resonating off each other like tuning forks. "At last!" she said, when the doorbell rang. "Why does he have to be so late?" She went out to the hall and I heard the bolts sliding across and then a man speaking. "There was a march on O'Connell Street," he said. "I was stuck on the bus for an hour."

"You could have got out and walked." That was Lou Anne against a backdrop of bolts.

"Well, I couldn't, could I? I hadn't rosary beads on me."

"Shh," Lou Anne said. "She's here."

He came to the door of the living room. "Why, hello," he said. "I didn't think you were arriving until later." He was short and slight, with dark hair and a dark beard. He wore a black leather jacket, and a satchel was slung over his shoulder, though he looked old for a student, late twenties or thereabouts.

"Daddy had to take calves to Tuam," I said, "so he dropped me to the bus early." Immediately, I regretted it, because why did this man need to know about our calves?

"It must be demanding for your father—the farm, I mean—now that your brother's gone to England."

I didn't like him knowing that about us. I wondered what else Lou Anne had told him.

"I'm Marcus," he said then, and he came over to the table and shook my hand. I wondered if I should tell him my name, or if he knew that, too, but he turned to Lou Anne, who was standing behind him. "How's she been today?"

"Oh, you know," Lou Anne said. "The same; she's been the same. I rang the surgery, but Dr. Raymond is still away and it's that locum doctor. You know what he's like."

"Did you tell him about her headaches?"

"He kept going on about getting her reading glasses. How many times do I have to tell you, I said to him, she doesn't read." She threw her hands up in disgust. "Does he even look at her file?"

"Should I try talking to him?" Marcus said.

"We can't fall out with him," Lou Anne said. "We might need a prescription before Dr. Raymond gets back. We'll have to muddle through until next week." She took the satchel from his shoulder. It was beaded with drops of rain, and she wiped it dry with the sleeve of her dress before hanging it on the back of a chair. She pushed a slick of wet hair out of Marcus's eyes and went to help him off with his jacket, which was wet, too, but he unzipped it himself and hung it beside the satchel. "I'll go fetch her for supper," he said, and he went upstairs.

Lou Anne stood for a moment, twisting her ponytail. Her gaze wandered absently around the room as if she'd been looking for something but had forgotten what. Her eyes came to rest on me, and she flinched, as if suddenly remembering I was there. "Get the napkins, would you?" she said, and she gestured to a mahogany dresser on the far side of the room. I located the napkins in the middle of a sea of crockery and knickknacks, and when Lou Anne didn't show any sign of doing anything with them, I placed one at each setting.

Marcus returned leading Cassie by the hand. She had on a blue quilted robe over her pajamas, buttoned to the neck. In her free hand was a glass jar with little black beads rattling about the bottom. She didn't come as far as the table but hung back a little, pulling at her plaits. "Cassie," Marcus said, "say hello to Louise," but she just stared. Marcus tried again. "Cassie," he said, but Lou Anne interrupted. "Oh, just leave it," she said. "She knows who it is. I've explained," and, pulling out a chair, she sat down and began to butter a slice of bread.

Marcus gave a little shrug and took a chair next to mine. Now that he was closer, I saw that his jumper was worn at the elbows and had a hole at the front that was unraveling. He patted the chair on the other side of him and Cassie sat down. She placed the jar in front of her on the table, and I saw that the black things weren't beads but a dozen or so dead wingless bluebottles. Marcus lifted the jar, put it on the floor beside Cassie's chair. She followed the back-and-forth of his knife as he cut her ham into small pieces, then did the same with her tomato. He took a forkful of food from his own plate and, nodding at Cassie, put it in his mouth. As if it were a signal she'd been waiting for, she picked up her own fork and did the same.

Marcus turned to me. "Which do you think you'll prefer?" he said. "English or French?"

And there it was again, another thing he knew about me. "English," I said. "I don't really like French."

He put down his knife and fork, regarded me with curiosity. "Why study it, then?"

"My mother thought it would be useful to have a foreign language. For teaching."

"So you want to be a teacher?"

Already I sensed it would be difficult to explain to Marcus how "want" had never been of much relevance in our house. "Yes," I said. "I do."

"I was a teacher once," Lou Anne said. "I taught English for a year in Spain. The school was right by the sea."

"Valencia," I said. "We have a postcard of it." On my mother's dressing table there was a dog-eared card slotted into the mirror, a scene of a ruined white-walled house surrounded by wild orange trees. It had been there for as long as I remembered, so long that I'd never inquired about who'd sent it.

"I can't believe your mother kept that," Lou Anne said.

"She was always too damn sentimental," but I could tell that she was pleased.

"A sentimentalist," Marcus said, "is one who desires to have the luxury of an emotion without paying for it."

I thought he was explaining for my sake and was offended, because I did know what the word meant, even if I couldn't have expressed it in that way.

"Marcus is studying philosophy at Trinity," Lou Anne said. "We're all the time reaping the benefits."

"That was Wilde, actually," Marcus said.

Now that Marcus had stopped eating, so had Cassie. She was fussing with her food, pushing pieces of ham to the edge of her plate, giggling when they toppled out onto the tablecloth. I waited for Lou Anne to correct her, but she didn't. Marcus rapped his knife gently against Cassie's plate—two sharp bell-like strikes as if he was about to make a speech—and she laughed. She picked up a piece of ham with her fingers and popped it into her mouth, continuing to giggle. She chewed with her mouth open, revealing a mess of pink masticated meat, so that we all looked to our own plates and the table grew quiet. Outside, a bus drew up, belched, hissed, and pulled away again, and as the last of the evening light settled upon the garden, I felt the first stirrings of a migraine.

MARCUS, I WOULD FIND out later, hadn't been to lectures in over a year and was no longer enrolled as a student at the college, though he did go there from time to time, taking his satchel of books with him. He didn't appear to have a job of any sort. The holed jumper had led me to believe his family was poor, but now I decided they were rich, the kind of rich where that sort of thing didn't matter. He'd been living in the house for almost three years, and Cassie adored him. The Wednesday of that first week, I came home from college to find them at the side of the house, bouncing a ball against the gable wall. Someone had laid a patio—a botch job, my father would have called it, because a number of paving slabs were missing and others were loose. Cassie was in a long red skirt and white turtleneck. Her hair was free of the plaits and swung about her shoulders as she chased after the ball. Sometimes she caught it, but mostly it bounced on past. The weather was unusually warm and dry for early October, and every time the ball hit the ground it sent up a little explosion of dust.

I slipped my rucksack from my back and, running over, positioned myself between Marcus and Cassie. The game grew faster, the smack of the ball against the wall louder, the clouds of dust thicker. Then Marcus launched the ball against the wall so hard that when it rebounded it flew past me, striking the fence behind, knocking over a terra-cotta planter. Cassie shrieked, clapped her hands to her face, then burst into laughter, and soon we were all laughing, staggering breathless around the garden. I stopped to wipe my eyes and, looking to the house, saw Lou Anne watching from a window set high in the gable wall. I looked at the smashed planter, split clean down the middle, the earth spilling out onto the grass. Lou Anne opened the window. "That fence is already on its last legs," she said. "Best not hurry it along." Marcus picked up his jumper from the grass and, without saying anything to either me or Cassie, went ahead of us into the house.

There was a morning, not long after, when the door of Cassie's room, usually kept closed, was open. Lou Anne was pulling sheets from the bed. "The district nurse is coming," she said, when she saw me in the doorway. "I wasn't expecting her until tomorrow but she rang to say her roster's changed." She looked drained. "Can I help?" I said. I expected her to say no, but she must have been especially tired, because she considered for a moment and said, "You could make the bed, I suppose." She pointed to a pile of folded clean linen. "Two sheets at least, and tuck them in properly, otherwise she'll only kick them off." Marcus had gone out earlier. From downstairs I could hear the blare of the TV, Cassie watching her cartoons at full volume. When Lou Anne went to let the nurse in, I took a quick look about the room. It was a mess, clothes stuffed untidily into a laundry basket, shelves upon shelves crammed with old biscuit tins, shoe boxes, jars full of mismatched beads and copper coins and buttons. Lou Anne, I'd discovered, had a high tolerance for disorder. Her own bedroom downstairs had once been part of the kitchen, and her belongings were constantly migrating from behind the makeshift partition: tights draped over the backs of chairs, hairbrushes with clumps of red hair left beside the stove.

The nurse was round cheeked and blushing. "From the country," Lou Anne whispered as we watched her lead Cassie away to be weighed on the bathroom scales. "She knows your mother's aunts from Claremorris." I'd finished dressing the bed, and, as I squeezed past Lou Anne to leave the room, I brushed against a tin on a lower shelf. The lid sprung open when it hit the floor, depositing a foul-smelling, ashlike substance onto the carpet. I bent to examine it and saw that it was the remains of dead insects, dozens and dozens of them, shriveled and desiccated. They could have been butterflies, or perhaps moths, because there were translucent slivers of what might once have been wings. Someone had pinned a number of specimens to a piece of board covered in green fabric, though only the furred barrels of their bellies remained.

"Quick," Lou Anne said, "before Cassie sees," and she dropped to her knees and began to scoop everything back into the tin. I joined in, but we weren't fast enough. Already the nurse and Cassie were returning from the bathroom, arms linked. Cassie gave a little wail. She pulled away from the nurse and, rushing forward, caught me by the shoulder. I toppled backward onto the carpet and then she was on top of me, pounding, pummeling, grabbing my hair. She took a fistful of the gritty powder and mashed it into my face, forcing it past my lips and in between my teeth. Lou Anne and the nurse were shouting and pulling at her, but she was stronger than either of them. Only when she shifted her weight did I manage to free one of my hands, and then I slapped her, hard, across the face. She stopped instantly, frozen. She stared at me in dismay, and then, as if all the rage had gone out of her, she collapsed onto my chest, hugging me and crying loudly.

Lou Anne and the nurse lifted her off me and sat her on the bed. She was still crying, and Lou Anne held her, tried to calm her, humming a verse of a song she liked, stroking her hair. I jumped up and ran to the bathroom. I spat in the sink, rinsed my mouth out under the tap, and spat again. I got my toothbrush and scrubbed my teeth, my tongue, the crevices at the back of my gums, until my spit turned pink and the inside of my mouth felt raw. When I'd finished, I realized that I was shaking, and I held on to the sink to steady myself. I heard Lou Anne and the nurse come out onto the landing, talking in low voices: "It's only going to get worse," the nurse said. "She's getting stronger all the time. How will you manage?"

"It wouldn't have happened if my other lodger was here," Lou Anne said. "He's very good with her, but he has to go to lectures on Wednesdays." I wondered why she bothered to lie to the nurse about Marcus, because what difference could it possibly make to the nurse if Marcus was at lectures or not? And then her voice dropped lower, but not low enough, and I heard her say: "She's been out of sorts lately,

since"—and here she paused—"since the change in our living arrangements."

I spent most of the day in my room, expecting Lou Anne
to come looking for me. That was what my mother did when
she and I fought, and I knew, without fully understanding
how it had come about, that Lou Anne and I were fighting. Midafternoon I went downstairs to make a sandwich. I
heard the crackle of Lou Anne's radio coming from behind
the draped fabric that separated her bedroom from the rest
of the kitchen. I boiled the kettle and rattled the lid of the
bread bin to let her know I was there, but she didn't come
out, and I took my sandwich back upstairs. Sometime after
nine P.M. that evening the doorbell rang and there was the
usual clamor of bolts. I'd dozed off, and now I sat up and
smoothed down my hair, arranged myself into what I imagined to be a more graceful pose. I heard Marcus and Lou
Anne talking first in the hall, then their voices fading as they
moved to the living room. After a while, I heard footsteps on
the stairs, then a knock on my door. "Come in," I said.

Marcus came in and stood beside my bed. For once, he
wasn't wearing the green jumper, but a red and blue checked
shirt that smelled of smoke. He picked up the book I'd been
reading, one from my college syllabus, and turned it over
to look at the cover. "Ah, yes," he said. "Rhys. What do you
think of her?"

"She's good," I said, carefully. There was more I could
have said: how all week I couldn't shift from my head the

images of Coulibri gone wild, the smell of dead flowers mingling with living ones; a poisoned horse beneath a tree, its eyes black with flies. But I'd learned to be wary when discussing books with Marcus. When I didn't say more, he sighed and closed the book, settled himself on the edge of the bed. "Lou Anne told me you hit Cassie today."

"She was on top of me," I said, "she was hurting me, and—"

He held up a hand. "You must never do that again," he said. "Never under any circumstances. Do you hear?"

"She could have killed me."

"It makes no difference what she does. You must never hit her."

All day I'd imagined the ways in which he might comfort me. Aggrieved by the unfairness of it all, I swung my legs over the other side of the bed and faced away from him. He reached across and rested a hand on my shoulder. "Listen," he said. "This is important. It mustn't happen again. Do you understand?"

I nodded without looking at him.

"Could you apologize, do you think?"

The idea didn't appeal to me. "She's asleep," I said.

"I meant would you apologize to Lou Anne."

"No," I said.

He sighed and got up, ran a hand through his hair. "All right," he said. "But can I at least tell her it won't happen again?"

"Tell her this," I said. I lifted my blouse and pointed to a

circle of bruised skin just below my ribs which, to my satis-
faction, was already darkening to purple. He came round to
my side of the bed and, swearing under his breath, stooped
to inspect it. I saw that his hair and the collar of his shirt
were damp, and thought that he must have walked from the
city center and that was why he was late. He went as if to
touch the bruise, but pulled back. "I'm damned if I need
any of this," he said, straightening up, and, without saying
anything more, he walked out of the bedroom. After he'd
gone, I tried to read a little more of my book, but couldn't.
I switched off the light and climbed fully clothed into bed. I
pulled the sheets over my face, frightened for the first time
of the moths that at night crashed headlong into the hot
bulb of my bedroom lamp, their blackened stumps scattered
across the floor in the mornings.

THE NEXT EVENING I ate in the college canteen and came
home as late as I dared. Even though I was being perfectly
quiet, Lou Anne put a finger to her lips as she let me in
and said, "Shh, she's asleep," as she secured the door. The
bolts, Marcus had explained, were on account of Cassie,
who sometimes wandered downstairs at night and had once
made her way onto the street. I presumed Lou Anne and I
were still fighting, but once she'd finished with the door she
said, "I'll make some tea," and disappeared into the kitchen.
I went into the living room and sat at the table. "Goodness,"
Lou Anne said, arriving back with a tray. "It's almost dark."

She put down the tray and moved about the room, switching on lamps. Her cheeks were flushed and I noticed that as well as the tea things, the tray held a small bottle of whiskey. She sat across from me at the table and poured tea into two mugs—the delicate china of that first evening had never again materialized. "Where's Marcus?" I said.

Lou Anne frowned. "How should I know?" she said. "He's a young man. I expect he's off doing whatever it is that young men do. Why should you or I worry our heads about him?" She leaned closer. "That's what women do," she said. "They do it all the time; they worry about men. We did it, your mother and I, we were fools for men." She splashed some whiskey into her tea, seemed to consider for a moment before offering me the bottle. When I shook my head, she dribbled a little more into her own cup. "You know what you need to do?" she said. "You need to make some friends instead of hanging out here every evening. You're young. This is your chance to have fun. If your mother was here, that's what she'd tell you."

I doubted this very much, but before I could say anything, Lou Anne got up and rummaged in a chest of drawers, tut-tutting in exasperation as she pushed aside old catalogs and oddments of fabric. She brought out a photo album. "I want to show you something," she said. Thumbing through the pages, she stopped at a photo. It took me a moment to realize it was of herself and my mother. It must have been taken in the years before my parents were married, because my mother was in a short skirt and was smoking a cigarette.

"You're the image of her," Lou Anne said, and, putting a finger to my chin, she tilted my face first one way then the other. "That day you arrived on my doorstep, it was like an apparition." She sighed and turned the page to another photo. This one was of Cassie when she was younger, standing with her hand outstretched. Spread across her palm, covering it almost entirely, was a red-and-blue butterfly, an enormous jewel of a thing, circles of silver dotted along the perimeter of its wings, a golden fuzz on its belly.

"Daddy ordered it through a catalog," Lou Anne said. "It came all the way from the Philippines. The stamps were almost as beautiful as the butterfly. I have them still."

I stared at the butterfly, imagined it plucked from the teeming colors of a rain forest, killed, boxed, and transported to a damp, muted house in Drumcondra.

"Cassie was very fond of Daddy," Lou Anne said. "He was always helping her with the butterflies. She misses him terribly."

Marcus arrived home just then. Lou Anne undid the bolts and let him in, and as soon as he entered the room I could tell that he'd been drinking. Lou Anne must have noticed, too, but she just poured some whiskey into a glass she took from the top of the dresser, a little gold-rimmed sherry glass, and handed it to him. He drank it back in one go, then, taking the bottle, poured himself another. He switched on the television and threw himself into an armchair. It was a motor-sports program, and the room filled with the waspish drone of racing cars. Lou Anne walked over to the TV and switched it off. "Give me a hand with this," she said, gesturing to the piano. I didn't know if she meant me or Marcus, but Marcus didn't stir, so I got up and began to help her move things. A jug I'd presumed empty turned out to contain stagnant water and the mulchy remnants of petals that sloshed over the sides when I lifted it. "Careful," Lou Anne said. "That piano's worth twenty grand." I froze, the jug in my hand, brown slime dripping onto the dark wood of the lid. From his armchair, Marcus began to laugh. I saw Lou Anne struggling to keep a straight face, then she laughed, too. "Don't you think I'd sell it if it was worth that?" she said, seating herself at the piano stool. "Look around you. Do you think there's anything here that I wouldn't sell if I could?"

"If I had money I'd go to Argentina," Marcus said. "A man from our town did that. You can get a thousand acres in Patagonia for the price of a hundred here. I'd never come back."

Lou Anne muttered something under her breath. She swept the last of the clutter from the piano onto the floor and raised the lid. I returned to the table. I didn't know enough to say whether her playing was any good; the piano was likely out of tune, and this may have been the reason for the brutish, slightly mutinous, notes. I did know that she couldn't sing: She struggled through a Bonnie Tyler song and a number of others I didn't recognize that were also beyond her capabilities. And then she stopped. She stood up without looking at either Marcus or me and carefully closed the lid before leaving the room. I heard her crossing the hall and going into the kitchen, and from there the footsteps fading as she went through to her bedroom.

Marcus sipped his whiskey and stared at me, and I stared back. A lamp on a table beside his armchair was angled toward his face, and with his dark hair and beard, his dark eyes, he looked like a figure from a Baroque painting, a Caravaggio Christ, luminous and reproachful. I had prepared what I'd say if he said anything more about hitting Cassie. He got up and came over to where I sat, bringing his glass of whiskey with him. He leaned down and kissed me, and I felt the coarse tickle of his beard, tasted the whiskey off his tongue. He put his glass down and pulled me to my feet, kissing me again, a longer kiss this time, his hands moving through my hair, sliding down along my neck to rest on my shoulders. I thought I heard a noise from the hall, and pulled away. He looked at me, questioningly.

"Lou Anne . . ." I said, inclining my head toward the door, but he just smiled. "Ah, my little Louise," he said. "Always such a worrier." He went to kiss me again, but paused. "You're called after her, aren't you?" he said. "I've only just realized. You're called after Lou Anne." This seemed to amuse him; he smiled and shook his head, then took me by the hand and, wordlessly, led me out to the hall and upstairs to my bedroom.

He pushed me down onto the bed and, removing his jeans and shirt, lay down beside me. As he unbuttoned my blouse, I listened for sounds from Cassie's room next door, or from Lou Anne's downstairs. He unhooked my bra and, raising himself on one elbow, stared at me for a moment before tracing a finger in slow circles around one of my nipples. I lay perfectly still as his finger trailed lower over my ribs, stopping at the patch of bruised skin that had darkened now to shades of blue and mauve. He put his mouth to it and kissed it. "Poor Louise," he said. "What was your mother thinking, sending you here?" His lips moved down along my stomach. He unbuttoned my jeans, tugged my knickers halfway down my thighs, and then I felt his mouth again, warm and wet, the busyness of his tongue. "Hush," he said when, forgetting myself, I made a noise, and then he reached for his jacket from the floor and took a square of foil from an inside pocket.

Afterward he talked about things he hadn't talked about before: his family—mostly his mother and younger sister, because his father was dead—who, it turned out, were living in Offaly, and who didn't appear to be in any way rich, but who ran a small grocery shop and farmed forty acres of land left to his sister by a grandmother.

"When do you visit them?" I asked, because it occurred to me that there had never been a weekend when he hadn't been at the house.

"I don't," he said.

I wondered how his mother allowed it. I had already made a visit home to Tuamgraney. "But they're your family," I said.

"What's family, when you think about it?" he said. "It's just something that happens to you; a bunch of people, not of your choosing, that you're forced into relationships with. I believe we have the right to choose our own families."

Your family was your family, I thought, and there was nothing you could do about it. I wanted to say this, but feared it might all have something to do with philosophy and then I would look foolish. I stroked the dark hair of his chest and stayed quiet.

"Do you know where I'd go if I could go anywhere I liked?" he said, and he began to talk again about Argentina. We had climbed under the bedclothes at this stage, and as he talked, his hand rested in the damp hollow between my legs, his fingers playing with me halfheartedly. I must have drifted off to sleep, because I woke sometime later to see him in the doorway, his profile briefly visible in the light from the landing as he pulled the door shut behind him.

SUNDAY MORNING, I FOUND Lou Anne and Marcus making sandwiches in the kitchen. Marcus looked up from slicing a block of cheese and said, "We're going to the lake, if you'd like to come."

"Why would she want to go to the lake?" Lou Anne said. "I wouldn't go myself, only I promised Cassie. It's madness, going this time of year—we'll catch our death of cold."

"It's not cold," Marcus said. He nodded to the window where a watery October sun was slanting through the blinds.

"I'd like to go," I said, before Lou Anne could say anything more. I was grateful, joyous even. Marcus had paid me

hardly any attention these past few days, even when I'd tried
to humor him by making an effort with Cassie.

Lou Anne got a flask from a cupboard and filled it with
boiling water. She began to add spoonfuls of instant coffee,
counting them under her breath.

"Have you got a swimsuit?" Marcus said.

"It's too damned cold for swimming," Lou Anne said,
putting the top on the flask. "Cassie will do her bit of pad-
dling, we'll eat our sandwiches, and we'll come home." She
packed the flask into a navy holdall on the kitchen table.

I had a red bikini that I'd bought the year before during
a shopping trip to Galway. It had journeyed from Galway
to Tuamgraney to Dublin without ever being worn, or being seen by my mother. I went upstairs and changed into
it, checked how it looked in the bathroom mirror. Good, I
thought, it looked good, and I put my clothes back on over it
and went downstairs.

I'd presumed that we would take a bus, but Lou Anne
had arranged the loan of a car, a little red Ford Fiesta. She
was driving, and Cassie was in the passenger seat, Marcus
and I in the back. A couple of cassette tapes were scattered
across the dash, and Lou Anne selected one that turned out
to be Debussy and put it on. It was lavish, ambiguous music,
and, as we proceeded down Drumcondra Road, the strange-
ness of the harmonies unsettled me, brought a feeling I was
unable to identify as one thing or another. I was holding a
tartan picnic rug on my lap, and Marcus slid his hand underneath, let it rest on my thigh. Lou Anne's driving was erratic:

She took corners too wide and too fast, went through a red light at a junction. The city was quiet that morning, mellow, the outlines of the trees softened by the scant yellowing leaves that still clung to their branches, and as we passed the cemetery an elderly man raised a hand in greeting, perhaps mistaking us for someone else.

We drove for an hour, maybe more, turning off the main road onto a narrower one, and farther on again, onto what was no more than a dirt track. Ahead of us was a lake, a dip scooped out of the surrounding farmland with a small woods at one end that stretched all the way down to the edge. Close to the shore, saplings had taken root in the lake bed, half-formed trees pushing up out of the water. When the dirt track petered out, we trundled downhill through a field. Lou Anne parked as close to the lake's edge as she could, so close that I feared if the hand brake didn't hold, the Fiesta might end up in the water.

We all climbed out and Lou Anne took the rug from me, snatched it away before I could offer to carry it. I went to lift the picnic basket from the boot, but she took that, too. The lake was gray and still, as black as onyx out at the center. Lou Anne spread the rug on a patch of grass and sat on it, looking out at the lake, the picnic basket unopened beside her. Cassie was already struggling out of her clothes, discarding them in a haphazard fashion for Marcus to gather up, until she was down to a navy one-piece. I noticed, and was ashamed of noticing, that her legs were heavily dimpled with cellulite and marked with long blue veins. Marcus had rolled up the ends of his trousers. He held out a hand to Cassie and motioned toward the water, but she crouched on the shingle. Scattered over the surface were dragonflies, all of them dead, felled perhaps by a recent turn in the weather, because even with the sunshine, it was colder here than in the city. She picked one up, but it came apart, leaving her holding only its leg. Scolding loudly, she began to gather others, arranging them in a line on top of a large stone.

I took off my shoes and socks, slid my jeans down to my ankles, and stepped out of them. I pulled my T-shirt over my head, the hairs on my arms standing up in little spiky forests. I was in only my bikini now, and I put one hand behind my back to check that the string was fastened. Without look-ing at Marcus, I walked the short distance to the water. The shingle hurt my feet, but I kept walking. The cold, when I waded in, was excruciating, but I steeled myself against it, kept walking out until the water lapped the top of my thighs and then I stopped, still with my back to him, to al-low him to look at me. I'd stubbed my toe on a stone and knew it must be bleeding, but I didn't care. I stood in the freezing water and let him look, while I stared across at the hills on the other side of the lake. The fields were better tended there, with fences, and a farmhouse standing in a clearing like something from a Constable painting. There was a pasture dotted with black-and-white cows, all so quiet and neatly ordered, tiny and far away. I dived down into the water, imagining how I would appear from the shore, the arc of my back, the red of the bikini against the white of my skin. I swam out farther, stopping to tread water somewhere around the middle. Only then did I look back.

Marcus was faced away from the lake, talking to Lou Anne. She was still sitting on the rug, fully clothed, with a towel wrapped around her shoulders. Cassie was a little farther off, scrabbling after her insects in the shingle. Marcus and Lou Anne were speaking in raised voices, but I was too far out to hear what was being said. All around me the water was black and still, and when I looked down at my feet they appeared white and ghostly. Back onshore, Marcus began to gesticulate. Lou Anne jumped to her feet, discarding the towel. She stood within inches of Marcus, waving her arms about, at one point shouting. Then she was walking away from him, breaking after a while into a run, getting smaller and smaller until she disappeared into the trees.

Marcus stared after her for a moment before turning, at last, to the lake. He stood with his hands on his hips, his gaze fixed on me as I continued to tread water. He stripped to his swim shorts, and waded in. As he swam, I watched his dark head approaching like an otter, and when he drew close, I turned and headed for the opposite bank. I stood in the shallows, waiting, like some creature emerged from the deep, water running in rivulets down my body. He scooped me up without saying anything and laid me down behind an evergreen bush that provided a screen of sorts. He struggled with the ties of my bikini top until, reaching behind, I undid it for him. He climbed on top of me then with none of the preamble of the last time and, pulling my bikini bottoms to one side, pushed into me, his mouth on mine, one hand kneading my breast. He thrust into me hard and fast, pressing me down into the mud, so that I imagined an indent forming like a worm cast that come winter would harden and fossilize. He groaned and collapsed onto my chest, and we lay there together, mud on my arms and between my legs, my hair glued into rope-thick strands, like a bird taken from an oil slick.

He pulled out of me suddenly, and, sitting up, he began putting back on his swim trunks. I sat up, too, noticing only then Lou Anne's voice coming from the other side of the lake. I looked about for my bikini top, found it floating at the water's edge. Marcus was halfway across by the time I'd tied the strings and set out after him. I could see Lou Anne up to her waist in the water. She was calling for Cassie and Marcus, and then Cassie again. Marcus reached her, took her by the arm, and dragged her to the shore. She tried to fight him off, but he gripped her by the shoulders. "Listen to me," he said. "She's not in the water. She wouldn't have gone in by herself, you know that."

"How do you know what she'd have done?" Lou Anne said, and she wrested herself free of him. "What makes you think you know anything about my daughter?" I had reached them now and stood shivering beside Marcus. Lou Anne waded past us, back into the lake, and thrashed to and fro, churning up the water until it grew brown and cloudy and it was impossible to see anything.

"She followed you into the woods," I said. While it had

formed as a half thought, a possibility, I knew as soon as I
had voiced it that this was what must have happened. Lou
Anne took off right away, running toward the trees. Marcus
and I struggled into our clothes and shoes and ran after her.
A short distance into the woods, the path split, one trail continuing on straight, the other leading uphill in a less defined
route. Marcus stopped, as did I, but Lou Anne carried on
uphill. "It has to be this one," she said. "I'd have seen her if
she took the other." Litter began to appear along the side of
the trail—empty crisp packets, dirty nappies—signs that we
were headed back toward the main road. The path widened,
became more defined, and I saw a brightness up ahead. No
one was talking now. Marcus and Lou Anne were in front,
behaving as if I weren't there. When Lou Anne's foot caught
on a tree root, Marcus reached out to steady her and she
took his hand, kept hold of it as they ran on. And then we
were out of the trees and standing on the hard shoulder of a
road, blinking in the sudden sunshine. It was the road we'd
driven down earlier before turning onto the dirt track, because I recognized a field that had caught my attention. It
was laid out like a gymkhana, and now a man was putting a
gray horse through its paces, riding it over a series of jumps
constructed from colorful poles.

"There she is!" Lou Anne said. I squinted and saw Cassie
some twenty yards away, just after the turnoff for the lake
where the main road disappeared around a bend. She was
a strange sight in her swimsuit, like something beached or
shipwrecked, a mermaid from a childhood story with her

fair hair loose around her shoulders. She had her back to us and was walking along the middle of the road, about to turn the corner. From that distance there was something stately about her, something ethereal, and as the light caught her hair she appeared almost transfigured. "Cassie!" Lou Anne shouted. She turned then, Cassie, and saw us. She didn't immediately come toward us, but she must have recognized us, because she waved. Lou Anne was still holding Marcus's hand, and in the field alongside, the man was still riding his horse, a steady drum of hooves fractured by small silences as he cleared each jump. A car came around the corner. It struck Cassie, tossing her into the air, her legs at a strange angle to her body. She landed on the car bonnet, where she traveled for a few yards before the car skidded to a halt, depositing her onto the road.

YEARS LATER, ON A trip home for a conference, I took a detour in a hired car and tried on impulse to find the lake, taking out the map provided by the rental company, guessing at the route we might have taken that day. Eventually I arrived at a pool of dark water that I knew wasn't it, but I stayed awhile nonetheless, and then, knowing I wouldn't try anymore, I drove back to the airport, gave back the car, and boarded my plane. I was teaching at a college in the American Midwest by then. Lou Anne had sold the house in Drumcondra the year after Cassie died and had bought a small house in County Clare. She was closer to my mother geographically now, but they rarely visited each other, although they continued to exchange Christmas cards. My mother said that Lou Anne asked after me in these, though I never pressed her on the details.

I moved out of the house in the weeks after the accident, as did Marcus, though he and I didn't keep in touch. I saw him once, a couple of years later, on a street in Temple Bar, clean shaven and in a suit. He was standing in the doorway of an office building with a number of other men in suits. He quickly looked at the ground as I passed, and I was glad that he did. It's rarely I think of him now, but to this day I can't hear Debussy without a tightening in my throat. Once, preparing to go into a meeting in Denver, I had to slip away to the restroom and lock myself in a cubicle for ten minutes having been ambushed by the piped Muzak of the elevator. What returns from time to time, though I wish it wouldn't, is that afternoon playing ball on the patio outside the house on Drumcondra Road. It lingers beneath the surface, quivering like a small but troublesome cyst. The dry October day, Cassie, the ball, the little clouds of dust; and Lou Anne looking down from the upstairs window, a sadness, a disappointment, in her face that at the time I attributed to the ruined terra-cotta planter, but which I now know was something else entirely.

IN THE ACT OF FALLING

——

IT WAS A LITTLE AFTER SEVEN A.M., AND OUTSIDE IN THE garden her nine-year-old son, Finn, was stringing a tennis net between two trees, stringing it not in the normal fashion, the way one might to play tennis, but horizontally, like a hammock. He was wearing a pair of too-short trousers, perhaps the trousers from last year's school uniform, and no shoes. The grounds on this side of the property were ragged but pretty, bounded by a low stone wall that allowed views across the fields to the gray slate roofs of Portlaoise. "I think it might've been a mistake to tell him about the ducks," Bill said.

"It's not about the ducks," she said. "If it wasn't the ducks, it would be something else."

They were having coffee in a room at the front of the house, a high-ceilinged, corniced room that she continued to think of as the dining room, though two years on, it remained unfurnished, apart from a small mahogany table they'd brought from their old house and two faux Queen Anne chairs. The room was long and narrow, with a south-facing bay window and another, smaller window overlooking the side garden, where their son was going back and forth between trees, checking and double-checking his knots. He'd found the net in the shed. It wasn't their net, though she supposed it must be now; it had come with the house, and had belonged to one or other of the people who had owned this place before them. Finn had commandeered it for the purpose of catching dead, or soon to be dead, birds. Birds, it seemed, were the next great heralds of the apocalypse, and Finn had decided it was important to catch them in the act of falling. Before the birds, there had been two long weeks of insects: a meticulous recording of spiders, flies, and beetles, tallies of the dead entered each night in a blue-lined copybook.

Bill left the window and came to sit beside her at the table. He was wearing an old shirt from his banking days—old but expensive, a Lanvin pinstripe with double cuffs, crumpled because he'd slept in it the night before—and a pair of tracksuit bottoms. He'd stopped getting his hair cut, and now it hung limp and slightly graying just below his ears.

"Will you take Finn to school today?" she said. It was half inquiry, half request.

"We'll see," he said. "We don't want to rush things, do we?"

He took one of the books from the floor beside his chair.

It was one she hadn't seen before, a hardback with a picture of an elaborately ornate Karyōbinga on the cover, and she looked away to spare herself seeing the price. They were all over the house, these books—and journals, too—little dog-eared towers of them in the bathroom and next to their bed, copies surfacing randomly on kitchen shelves and windowsills. They were about art, mostly: Oriental art, Japanese antiquities, Muromachi paintings, wooden carvings detailed with gold leaf and lacquer. They were the kind of books she might once have bought for herself, books she could still possibly take pleasure in were they not so hideously expensive.

"It's been almost a month," she said. "He needs to go back to school. His suspension ended over a week ago."

Bill didn't answer immediately. Instead, he turned a page with ceremonial reverence, lifting the glossy paper, letting it fall, smoothing a hand across a monotone print depicting a line of leafless trees fronting a temple. "I don't think he's ready," he said. He gestured toward the garden, where Finn was leaning into the net, resting his weight on it, testing it. "Look at him. Isn't he happy?"

Her coat was on the back of her chair, and she took it, draped it across her shoulders. It was cold, this room, even in April, even with the chimney blocked up and insulating tape sealing the splintered frames of the sash windows—the original windows, as the auctioneer had pointed out, practically salivating at the sheer oldness of it all, as she had, too, back then. It was easier for Bill if Finn didn't go to school, she thought—that way he didn't have to walk with the child to the bus stop and then ride the bus with him into town, didn't have to make his way back only to repeat the journey when school finished in the afternoon.

"Astonishing, when you consider it," he said. "The deep recession into space."

"Sorry?" she said, before realizing that he was talking about something in the book. He was off then, feeding her random pieces as he read, while she ate a slice of toast and drank her coffee. Above the table, a lead-crystal chandelier hung like a tree in winter, most of its pendants missing. She should take it down and be done with it, she thought. She should put it out in the shed with the rest of the rubbish and pick up something in IKEA. She'd imagined a life for the people who'd lived here before, had pieced it together from the things they'd left behind—the skeleton of a pony trap, its metal spine rusting at the back of the shed, the stone hot-water jars. But it occurred to her now that perhaps she'd gone about it wrong, that perhaps they were not to be known by what they left but by what they took, in which case she would never know them. Outside the window, Finn was throwing stones of varying size into the center of the net. "If you do decide to take him to school," she said, "I found his school tie when I was tidying the playroom. It's hanging in his wardrobe."

"Okay," he said, without looking up, and she knew there would be no school for Finn today.

* * *

THIS IS WHAT SHE'D told Finn about the ducks: Yesterday, in Stephen's Green, the ducks on one of the ponds had died, the smaller pond with the gunmetal green railings by the side exit to the shopping center—not one or two of the ducks but all of them. She'd seen them as she cut through the park on her way to the office, stopping where a small crowd had gathered. And Bill was right—it was no story for a child, especially not this child, so sensitive that sometimes she thought the very passage of air around him might strip the skin off him. But she'd arrived home late, and tired, and, on entering the kitchen and seeing them together in easy silence at the table, she'd felt a need to announce herself, to offer something that might allow access to their world. And so she'd unleashed it, the story of the ducks, how some were almost wholly submerged, just the tip of a wing or a tail feather breaking the surface of the water, while others lay on the muddy bank, their jeweled heads pressing beak-shaped indents into the silt. One had made it onto the grass and lay toppled beneath the spiked branches of a hawthorn bush, and she knew that if she touched it, it would still be warm. All the time she was talking, Finn was looking at her, and she could almost hear the thoughts whirring inside his head. Bill had raised an eyebrow as he dished out mashed potatoes and peas, the only dinner that Finn could be persuaded to eat. She'd looked toward the oven to see if perhaps he had cooked something else for her. He'd followed her gaze. "I could do you an egg if you like," he'd said.

"It's okay," she'd said. "This is fine." She would like to

know how exactly Bill passed his days, but this mystery was as unfathomable to her as the lives of the house's previous inhabitants. It was not as if he spent much time on home maintenance. He'd had business cards printed advertising his services as a financial consultant, but thus far no clients had materialized. She'd taken a seat opposite Finn at the kitchen table and watched him eat his food the way he always did: peas first, one by one, then the potatoes, all the time his small brow furrowed with such intensity that she imagined the ducks resurrected inside his head, waddling crookedly, beating their wings against the walls.

SHE SLIPPED HER ARMS into her coat, took her briefcase from the hall, and went outside to where her car was parked in front of the house. "Bye, Finn," she called, and raised her hand in a wave. He waved back, then returned to the task of untying one of the strings. Setting down her briefcase, she crossed the lawn, the heels of her shoes sinking into the damp ground, and stopped beside the net. For a moment, she considered what it might be like to climb onto it, to close her eyes, to sleep. Finn had managed to work the string loose, and now he was circling the tree with it again, but at a point higher up, round and round, preparing to refasten it. He stopped when it would go no farther, and began to tie a knot. "Here," she said, "let me do that."

"It has to be a pipe-hitch knot," he said. "Can you do a pipe hitch?"

She shook her head. "I'd better leave you to it, then," she said. Sheets of paper were spread out on the grass. Stooping to get a better look, she saw that they were covered in complex, intricate diagrams, the margins scribbled with words like "plague" and "apocalypse" and little hand-drawn pictures of birds, small, fat-bellied things with disproportionately long legs and large feet. Among the drawings was a copy of a magazine, a publication brought to the house from time to time by a preacher woman. She was one of the few people who braved the muddy lane to visit them or, more precisely, to visit Bill and Finn, because she always called in the daytime.

"Was the preacher here?" she said, picking up the magazine.

"You mean Molly?"

Since when was he on first-name terms with the preacher woman? "Is that what she's called?"

"Yes." He'd completed the knot and was tugging on the ends to see if it would hold.

"So when was Molly here?"

"Yesterday. But she couldn't stay long. She had to go visit a woman who's come all the way from Virginia to live up by the lake." Satisfied with the knot, he turned to his mother. "Virginia is a girl's name," he said, "but it's also a place in America. The first peanuts ever grown in America were grown in Virginia, but now the people of Virginia mostly grow tobacco, which is immoral and also causes plagues."

"What's Molly like?" she said, conscious that she should

be on the road already. Delay would be paid for at an extortionate rate; ten minutes could cost her an hour if she hit the M50 at the wrong time.

Finn considered for a moment. "You know Sally, the horse trainer on *Blue Mountain*?"

"*Blue Mountain*? Where's that?"

"It's a TV program."

When she shook her head, he tried again. "You know Princess Karla from *The Jupiter Gang*?"

What on earth were these programs that Bill was letting him watch? She would book a day off next month, she decided; even a half day would do. She would make an appointment with the school principal, she would ring a child psychologist, she would return the calls of that woman from the bank. There was no longer any reason to hope Bill might do these things.

Finn had his eyes screwed up, concentrating. "You know Angelina Jolie?" he said.

Goodness, she thought, this Evangelical was not what she had in mind. What she had in mind—an image she knew to be stereotypical, ridiculous—was a middle-aged matronly woman in homely dress, nineteenth-century Mormon meets Catholic nun, with gray hair in a bun and mannish lace-up shoes. "Yes," she said. "I know Angelina Jolie. Is that who she's like?"

"Sort of," he said. "She's got hair like her, and eyes like her, but she's not as tall. And her skin is more tanned."

It was nonsensical to be jealous of a woman who had

made it her life's purpose to decry pride and vanity and sins of the flesh, to decry most things, if the magazines she brought were anything to go by. She went to put the magazine in her briefcase, but the boy snatched it from her and, going a little distance away, settled himself cross-legged in the grass. She watched him as he read: such a serious child; serious, fervent, and, though it pained her to admit it, strange. She went over and stood beside him.

"We are living in the last of days," he said, without looking up. "Soon, the armies of the Beast will come and there will be pestilence and lakes of fire."

"Give me that," she said, reaching for the magazine, but he was too quick for her. Jumping up, he took off to the far end of the garden, pages fluttering in his hand as he ran. She looked at her watch: There was no time to go after him. "I'll see you this evening," she called as she walked back across the grass to her car.

She drove down the avenue, swerving around the deepest of the potholes, slowing through the shallower ones. On her right, in contrast to the mossy stone wall, a crude post-and-rail fence separated their property from the wasteland next door, which had once formed part of the house's extensive grounds. A developer, having no use for the house itself, had fenced it off and sold it, together with an acre of garden. When she and Bill had first viewed it, there had been a pair of tall wrought-iron gates at the end of the avenue, but by the time they moved in, the gates were gone, taken, she'd learned later, by a creditor of the builder. The wasteland was meant to be Phase 2 of a development of three-bed semis. Last winter, a storm had felled the advertising hoardings along the perimeter and now they lay half buried in the grass, their peeling fragments of swings and smiling lovers and flower beds like remnants of an ancient mosaic. Phase 1 was a field distant, a ghost estate already sliding into dereliction. She'd heard that a few of the houses were occupied, despite being without plumbing or electricity, and once, when she'd crossed the wasteland to peer through the fence, she'd seen a van parked outside one and a mound of garbage bags outside another.

Three weeks ago, during geography class, Finn had struck the boy who sat beside him full square on the mouth. "For no apparent reason," according to the headmaster, though it later transpired that the boy had put his hand on Finn's arm to stop him jigging it up and down. "That constituted assault," Bill said. "Finn was acting in self-defense."

"They're nine-year-old boys," she'd said. "Can we stop talking about them like they're on indictment?" There had, apparently, been a lot of blood, a degree of panic, and a lost tooth, though it turned out that the tooth was a milk tooth and would have been lost anyway. "Hardly the point," the headmaster had said when Bill offered this, and she couldn't help thinking that the suspension might have been one week rather than two had she gone on her own.

✿ ✿ ✿

AT MIDDAY SHE TOOK her lunch to the park. The day was cool, with barely any sun, and there were plenty of benches free. She chose one beneath a tree and unwrapped her sandwich. A van from the Parks Department pulled up beside the small pond and reversed onto the grass. A warden got out and, going around to the back of the van, unbolted the doors and let down the ramp. From where she sat, she could hear him making a series of cooing, coaxing noises. Eventually, a duck plodded out, dazedly, as if the van were a hard-shelled futuristic egg from which it had just hatched. It stood, bemused, on the ramp for a moment, and then suddenly there were more ducks behind it, pushing and jostling, and it was too late for it to turn back. A dozen of them, maybe more, descended onto the grass, a mix of lustrous greens and blues and mottled browns, and as the warden herded them toward the water, a child began to throw bread, striking one of them on the head. The warden shooed them onward, and they were wading in now, swimming, moving in tight little circles before broadening their orbit.

They should have made her happy, but they didn't. They were indistinguishable from the ducks that had died the day before. If she hadn't cut through the park yesterday morning, if she hadn't taken lunch here today, she might even have thought, next time she visited, that they were the same ducks. There was trickery of a sort at work, a sleight of hand that suggested that the first ducks had never existed, and only she alone, in silent witness, knew better. She put the remainder of her sandwich in the trash bin and, leaving the park, made her way back to her office. Later, at her computer, she typed "Stephen's Green ducks dead" into a search engine, but her inquiry yielded nothing of relevance.

SHE WAS DRIVING HOME shortly after six P.M., with the radio set to a music station. She liked this stretch of the commute, the city traffic behind her, the winding country roads that led into Portlaoise then out of it again. There was a particular house that drew her eye each evening, a house of the same period and style as their own early nineteenth-century Georgian, but better tended. In winter, candles in glass jars hung from holly trees, and now, in late spring, daffodils bloomed on either side of the long avenue. This evening as she drove past, she felt not inspired but admonished. If it was still light by the time they finished dinner, she would attempt a cleanup of the beehives in the southwest corner of their property. She would ask Finn to help her; it might take his mind off all things dead. They could paint the hives different colors, use them as planting boxes; she had no desire to keep bees. Items of beekeeping equipment—a suit, a veiled hat, a smoker—had been among the things left behind in the shed, and she'd taken this as evidence that the people who had lived here before were beekeepers, but perhaps it was better evidence that they were not; that they were, at best, failed beekeepers. And for no reason that she could point to, she knew the beekeeping paraphernalia hadn't belonged to the same person who owned the pony trap; these things, she was sure, were the leavings of two different people, the discarded parings of two separate lives.

It had rained earlier in the afternoon, a light drizzle, and the three steps that led to the front door were slippery. Above the door, just below the box that housed the burglar alarm, was a domed copper bell. The rope pull was missing, but the metal tongue remained, and she was still startled occasionally, in strong winds, by a shrill, high note. Letting herself into the hall, she thought she detected the smell of something cooking, something other than potatoes and peas. Bill came out of the kitchen to greet her. "Guess what?" he said. "I've got an interview."

"That's great," she said, trying not to look too surprised, because she'd begun to suspect that he no longer applied for jobs. "What's it for?"

"A position at the museum in Athy."

"The museum?" she said, puzzled. "You mean in the accounts department?"

"It's more hands-on," he said. "Cataloging exhibits, working on the archives, that sort of thing."

Careful, she warned herself, careful how you play this. Mentally, she had already begun to calculate the cost of his return bus fare, adding to it the cost of new work clothes, the cost of paying someone to mind their son. To buy a little time, she busied herself with hanging her coat on a peg and then, turning to him again, said: "Where's Finn?"

"He's in the kitchen," Bill said, "worrying about ducks."
He began to walk back down the hall, and she followed him.
"So how much does the job pay?" she asked, doing her best
to sound casual.

"They said we can discuss salary at the interview."

"But they do actually pay?"

"Of course." He halted in the doorway of the kitchen and
frowned. "You could try to sound more pleased," he said.
"You wanted me to get a job. Well, that's what I'm doing."

She felt like telling him that this had nothing to do with
want—that what either of them might have wanted had
stopped being relevant a long time ago. "Sorry," she said, "I
just . . . you know . . . when is the interview?"

"Tomorrow at four. Which means I'll need to leave here
just after three."

"But who will look after Finn?"

"I thought you could take the afternoon off."

"I have appointments," she said. "If I'd had more notice . . ." She saw then that Finn was sitting at the kitchen
table, and that the thing he had on a plate in front of him,
which at first glance she'd taken for a soft toy, was in fact a
dead bird. Easy does it, she told herself, Deep breaths. She
went over and stood beside him. He looked up from poking
the bird with a fork, and smiled. It was small and dark, with
black and brown feathers, its pinkish claws curled. "Did you
catch it in your net?" she said. She pictured it dropping from
the sky, the taut bounce as it rose only to fall back again.

"No," he said. "I found it by the river."

She watched as he plucked a feather from the bird's belly. "What are you doing?" she said. "It might be diseased."

"It *is* diseased," he said. "It's got plague." He was pulling out feathers in swift sharp yanks, leaving a clearing of pink-hued skin bubbled with goosebumps. He picked up a knife and prodded the cleared patch as if about to make an incision. "Okay," she said. "That's enough, get it off the table right now." Behind her, Bill was taking something from the oven. It was the first time he had cooked properly in weeks. She watched as he peeled the foil cover from a roasting tin, and when the rush of steam dispersed, she saw that it was a chicken.

After dinner, Bill disappeared into the room off the kitchen that they used as a TV room. She had abandoned the idea of interesting Finn in the beehives: He'd eaten his potatoes and peas, then taken the feathered cadaver outside to the garden, where he sat examining it, so engrossed that she hadn't the heart to take it from him. She did the dishes before joining Bill in the TV room. It was a small space that might once have been a maid's room and was easier to heat than the larger rooms in the front. Bill was sitting in an armchair, toasting his socked feet on the bars of an electric fire.

The husband of one of her colleagues had taken a job in Dubai last year. It was difficult, of course, her colleague had said, but every second month she left the kids with her mother and flew out for a week. In three years' time they would be back on their feet; it would be worth it. Looking at Bill now, sitting there reading one of his art journals, she wished that he would go to Dubai, too; it shocked her, the force with which she wished this, as did the composure with which she found herself contemplating it. She went to a cupboard and took out the bottle of brandy left over from Christmas, poured a measure for herself, another for him. He took the glass from her, but said nothing.

"Maybe you could take Finn with you tomorrow?" she said.

He looked up from his journal. "Turn up with a kid in tow? I might as well not bother."

And she saw now how this would unfold, how any time in the future she hinted he should get a job, it would come back to this: He'd wanted to, he'd tried, she'd thwarted it. She took a mouthful of brandy. "I think you should go," she said.

"What about your appointments?"

"I can't get out of the first one, but I'll ask someone to cover the later ones. Put on one of Finn's DVDs for him. I'll be home by three-thirty P.M."

"You mean leave him on his own?"

She was tempted to say it wouldn't be much different from any other day. As best she could tell, Bill mostly seemed to leave the boy to his own devices.

"It's only for half an hour," she said. "He'll be fine. Give him his lunch before you go."

"I give him his lunch every day," he said. He was silent

for a moment, and then he said: "You really think I should go?"

"Yes," she said. "I do."

"Okay, then," he said. "I will."

THE PONY TRAP HAD most likely belonged to a woman called Eliza Harriet Smithwick, who, according to the title deeds, had been granted a life interest in the house and a hundred acres as part of a marriage settlement in 1886. An ancestor of hers had acquired the land from the Earl of Mountrath for the princely sum of eighty pounds, ten shillings. Oh, how she and Bill had laughed with the solicitor about that—eighty pounds, ten shillings!—because it was possible for anything to be funny in those days, anything at all. They'd bought in those last few weeks before the crash, when the market, like a ball in flight, had quietly, imperceptibly, stopped rising, had hung for a millisecond at the peak of its trajectory before it began to drop.

She was thinking about this as she drove too fast up the avenue the following evening, her knuckles white on the steering wheel. It was just after five-fifteen P.M. Nobody had been able to cover her appointments, or, more accurately, nobody had been willing to. It was like that at work lately: everybody pretending busyness, everybody watching, the way children in a parlor game watch the chairs, knowing that the music could stop at any moment. Bill had telephoned at two, inquiring as to the whereabouts of a particular blue shirt. "Be sure to lock the doors," she'd said, to which he'd replied that he always locked them, this being a downright lie. She didn't tell him that she'd be late.

As it turned out, the front door was locked. Stepping into the hall, she heard canned laughter and the soundtrack of a cartoon. "Hey, Finn," she called, putting down her briefcase. She hung up her coat and looked into the TV room. A plate of peas was abandoned on the floor beside the armchair. A DVD was playing, but the room was empty. "Finn?" she called again. "Finn, sweetheart, Mom's home." He wasn't in his bedroom, either. She went from room to room upstairs, then downstairs again, where, in the dining room, she noticed the curtains moving and saw that the window was open.

She continued to call his name as she circled the house and garden. She climbed through the post-and-rail fence into the wasteland next door. From where she stood, she could see as far as the rough track that ran along the river, and, in the next field, the rows of unfinished houses. She cupped her hands around her mouth. "Finn!" she shouted.

A man was walking at speed along the track, breaking now and again into a run. He veered off and came toward her, his head bent, his hands in the pockets of his anorak. He was in his thirties, she guessed, with straggly brown hair and a reddish-brown beard, a colony of pimples on one cheek. "I heard you calling him," he said. "I know where he is."

"Where?" she said.

"Over there." He pointed to the houses. "I seen him earlier." His anorak was torn, and he was wearing dirty gray trainers and no socks.

"Thank you," she said curtly. She took a step forward, but he remained positioned in front of her.

"I seen you going off in your car sometimes," he said. "In the mornings."

She wondered if this was an attempt to intimidate her, but he was grinning, the grin open and a little vacuous, and she decided he was probably harmless. "Yes," she said, "that's right. I work in the city." She stepped around him and walked quickly in an effort to put some distance between them, picking her way over a coil of discarded wire that wound snakelike through the grass. He caught up and walked alongside, so close that his arm brushed against hers. She would run to one of the occupied houses if he got awkward, she decided; she was nearer to them now than she was to her own house.

"Through here," the man said. He had scurried ahead and was pulling wide an opening in the chain-link fence. He was as eager as a child, smiling as he held the mesh open, and she noticed how his wrists were frail and thin and scarred. She stooped to fit through the gap, and as she did she felt his hand, briefly, on the small of her back. In the next field, dozens of houses stretched out in front of her. Most of the windows had been smashed, and they stood blind in the late-afternoon light, surrounded by weeds and litter. There, still, were the refuse sacks she remembered from before, but there was no van, nothing to suggest that anyone was living here. The man led her across ground strewn with cans and broken glass to a house in the middle of a row. "In here," he said, climbing over a window ledge, but she shook her head. The earth beneath the ledge was churned up, indented with footprints of various sizes. "Where's my son?" she said.

The man was standing in what had likely been intended as a sitting room. The floor was rough concrete, and seeds blown into crevices had taken root, weeds pushing up through cracks. She saw in one corner a mug that belonged to Finn and next to it the jacket her sister had given him for his birthday. How long had he been coming to this place? she wondered. How long had he been hanging out with this man? Because the man's belongings were here, too—clothes, cardboard boxes, a sleeping bag—all piled in the center of the room. She took a deep breath. "You told me you saw him," she said. "Now can you please tell me where he is?"

He picked up a metal rod from a pile of rubbish and struck it on the floor a couple of times. Swinging it back and forth, he crossed the room to the fireplace. She saw then that a thing she had taken for a bundle of rags was a dog stretched out, dead, its head at an odd angle to its body. There was a large bald circle on its back and, in the center of the circle, a wine-colored spot, like a birthmark, fading into softer reds and pinks as it radiated outward. Gripping the rod in both hands, the man raised it high, then brought it down again, piercing the dog through the stomach.

"Where is he?" she screamed, banging the window ledge with her fist. "What have you done with him?"

He stared at her blankly and rubbed the back of one hand across his eyes, as if he'd just woken. "He was here this morning," he said.

She turned and ran, back to the gap in the fence, tripping on the way, falling and tearing her tights. Her hands were shaking as she struggled to part the wire mesh and squeeze through. When she'd gone a little distance, she stopped to catch her breath. She looked behind to see if the man was following, but there was no sign of him. She stood for a moment and tried to think what to do. It was possible that while she'd been here, Finn had returned home, had climbed back in through the window and was there now, waiting for her, or for his father, who would be home shortly. It was also possible that he was down by the river, searching for dead things, so absorbed in his activities that he hadn't heard her. Other possibilities crowded in on the heels of these, but she pushed them aside. She looked toward their house and saw it as a stranger might: an abandoned outpost, stately but diminished, plundered. The sun had moved lower in the sky, and now it caught the glass of the windows, causing them to blaze as if they'd been set alight. For a moment she imagined she saw the face of a woman pressed against a pane. What became of Eliza Harriet Smithwick? she wondered, and what would she think if she saw what had been done to her house and her gardens? She became aware of a stinging pain in her leg and, looking down, noticed that her knee was bleeding. "Finn!" she shouted.

And then she heard it: a yell, a small, joyous bellow of

trumpeting delight that was her son's voice, coming from the direction of the river. She turned and saw him cresting the grassy embankment above the water, sun reflecting off the near-white blond of his hair. She began to run toward him. He had a stick in his hand, and he was waving it in the air like a sword and making whooping noises. She was within a dozen yards of him before she realized he was not alone. Lying on the grass, reading, was a slim, tanned woman of about thirty. Sunlight filtered through the trees, parting the shadows along the bank, streaking her long hair. The woman raised her eyes from a book. It was a Bible bound in brown leather, and, before she closed it and sat up, she marked her page with a yellow ribbon. "Hello," she said, shading her eyes with her hand. "Isn't it a glorious day? We thought it a shame to stay indoors." Finn waved to his mother but didn't go to her. He seated himself next to the woman and picked up a magazine from a pile on the ground.

Was it possible they could have been here all this time and not heard her calling? She was conscious of her torn tights, her bleeding leg, the incongruity of her tailored jacket and pencil skirt, here where everything was peaceful, where sunlight dappled her child's blond head and weeds in flurries of blue and white bloomed along the riverbank. She crouched beside her son and hugged him. "Finn," she said, "I was so worried about you." He smiled but, shrugging away her arms, continued to read. Not knowing what to do, she settled herself next to him, tucking her legs underneath her to hide the bloodied knee. The preacher woman's legs were bare, she noticed, bare and brown. She wondered if Finn had simply climbed out the window to the woman or if she, before luring him Pied Piper style across the fields, had climbed in. She pictured her going from room to room, sitting at the mahogany table under the ravaged chandelier, her green catlike eyes that, yes, were ridiculously like Angelina Jolie's, taking in all the brokenness.

"We come down here sometimes when the weather is good," the woman said. "Finn knows the names of everything—insects, birds, plants. He's a walking encyclopedia."

Stay away from my son, she wanted to say. Stay away from him with your beasts and your lakes of fire and your pestilence. Instead, she said: "Yes, he's an exceptionally bright child." And because in the silence that followed it seemed that something more was expected of her, she gestured to a cluster of purple flowers with yellow hearts that grew a few feet away. Possibly, they were violets; she had never been good with plants. "They're beautiful, aren't they?" she said.

The woman smiled. She picked up her Bible, opening it not to the place she had marked but to a different page, and began to read. "Consider the lilies of the field," she said, "how they grow; they toil not, neither do they spin: and yet I say unto you, that even Solomon in all his glory was not arrayed like one of these." There was a soft swishing sound, the sound of someone moving through long grass. Bill was making his way toward them across the wasteland, his jacket thrown over one shoulder, his gait relaxed, unhurried. "Dad!" Finn shouted, and he jumped up and ran to his father.

She kept her eyes on her husband until she knew he was near enough to have seen her, and when he didn't wave or call out, she turned away. She lay back on the grass and looked up. A flock of small birds, starlings perhaps, were flying in an arrow formation above the trees. As she watched, they drew close together to form a dark, quivering orb. For a moment, they appeared freeze-framed as if someone had pressed Pause, and, just as she thought that they would surely fall, they scattered like gunshot across the evening sky.

DINOSAURS ON OTHER PLANETS

FROM THE FENCE BEHIND THE HOUSE, KATE COULD SEE her husband up at the old forestry hut where mottled scrub-land gave way to dense lines of trees. "Colman!" she called, but he didn't hear. She watched him swing the ax in a clean arc and thought, from this distance, he could be any age. Lately, she'd found herself wondering what he'd been like as a very young man, a man of twenty. She hadn't known him then. He had already turned forty when they met.

It was early April, the fields and ditches coming green again after winter. Grass verges crept outward, thickening the arteries of narrow lanes. "There's nothing wrong," she shouted when she was still some yards off. He was in his shirtsleeves, his coat discarded on the grass beside him. "Emer rang from London. She's coming home."

He put down the ax. "Home for a visit, or home for

good?" He had dismantled the front of the hut and one of the side walls. The frame of the old awning lay on the grass, remnants of green canvas still wound around a metal pole. On the floor inside, if "floor" was the word, she saw empty beer cans, blankets, a ball of blackened tinfoil.

"Just for a few days. A friend from college has an exhibition. I wasn't given much detail. You know Emer."

"Yes," he said, and frowned. "When is she arriving?"

"Tomorrow evening, and she's bringing Oisín."

"Tomorrow? And she's only after ringing now?"

"It'll be good to have them stay. Oisín has started school since we last saw him." She waited to see if he might mention the room, but he picked up the ax, as if impatient to get back to work.

"What will we do if the Forestry Service come round?" she said.

"They haven't come round this past year. They don't come round when we ring about the drinking or the fires." He swung the ax at a timber beam supporting what was left of the roof. There was a loud splintering but the beam stood firm, and he drew back the ax, prepared to strike again.

She turned and walked back toward the house. The Dennehys, their nearest neighbors, had earlier that week sown maize, and a crow hung from a pole, strung up by a piece of twine. It lifted in the wind as she walked past, coming to rest again a few feet from the ground, above the height of foxes. When they first moved here, she hadn't understood that the crows were real, shot specially for the purpose, and had asked Mrs. Dennehy what cloth she sewed them from, while the Dennehys' two sons, then just young boys, sniggered behind their mother's back.

After supper, she took the duvet cover with the blue teddy bears from the airing cupboard and spread it out on the kitchen table. The cat roused itself from the rug by the stove and went over to investigate. It bounded in one quick movement onto a chair and watched, its head to one side, as she smoothed out creases. There were matching pillowcases, and a yellow pajama holder in the shape of a rabbit. Colman was at the other side of the kitchen, making a mug of Bovril. "What do you think?" she said.

"Lovely."

"You couldn't possibly see from that distance," she said.

"It's the same one as before, isn't it?"

"Well, yes," she said. "But it's a while since they visited. I'm wondering, is it a bit babyish?"

"You're not going to find another between now and tomorrow," he said, and she felt the flutter in her eyelid start up, the one that usually preceded a headache. She had hoped the sight of the duvet cover might have prompted an offer to move his stuff, or at least an offer to vacate the room so that she could move it. "It'll be an improvement on that brown eiderdown, anyway," she said. "John was still at school when we bought that," but he just drank his Bovril and rinsed the mug, setting it upside down on the draining board. "Good night," he said, and went upstairs. The cat jumped down from the chair and padded back across the kitchen to resume its position on the rug.

NEXT MORNING, SHE STARTED with his suits. She waited until he'd gone outside, then carried them from John's old room to their bedroom across the landing. The wardrobe there had once held everything, but now when she pushed her coats and dresses along the rail they resisted, swung back at her, jostling and shouldering, as if they'd been breeding and fattening this past year. For an hour she went back and forth between the rooms with clothes, shoes, books. The winter before last, Colman had brought the lathe—a retirement gift from the staff at the co-op—in from the shed and had set it up in their son's room. He would turn wood late into the night and often, when she put her head around the door in the morning, she would find him, still in his clothes, asleep on John's old single bed. There began then the gradual migration of his belongings. He appeared to have lost interest in the lathe—he no longer presented her with lamps or bowls—but for the best part of a year, he had not slept in their bedroom at all.

Colman had allowed junk to accumulate—magazines, spent batteries, a cracked mug on the windowsill—and she got a sack and went around the room, picking things up. The lathe and wood turning tools—chisels, gouges, knives—were on a desk in the corner, and she packed them away in a box. She put aside Colman's pajamas, and dressed the bed with fresh linen, the blue teddy bears jolly on the duvet, the rabbit propped on a chair alongside. Standing back to admire it, she noticed Colman in the doorway. He had his hands on his hips and was staring at the sack.

"I haven't thrown anything out," she said.

"Why can't the child sleep in the other room?" He went over to the sack, dipped a hand in, and took out a battery.

"Emer's room? Because Emer will be sleeping there."

"Can't he sleep there, too?"

She watched him drop the battery back into the sack and root around, a look of expectancy on his face, like a boy playing lucky dip. He brought out the cracked mug, polished it on his trousers, and then, to her exasperation, put it back on the windowsill.

"He's six," she said. "He's not a baby anymore. I want things to be special; we see so little of him." It was true, she thought, it was not a lie. And then, because he was staring at her, she said, "And I don't want Emer asking about . . ." She paused, spread her arms wide to encompass the room. "About this." For a moment he looked as if he were going to challenge her. It would be like him, she thought, to decide to have this conversation today, today of all days, when he wouldn't have it all year. But he picked up his pajamas and a pair of shoes she had missed beneath the bed and, saying nothing, headed off across the landing. Later, she found his pajamas folded neatly on the pillow on his side of the bed, where he always used to keep them.

✤ ✤ ✤

COLMAN WAS ON THE phone in the hall when the car pulled up in front of the house. Kate hurried out to greet them and was surprised to see a man in the driver's seat. Emer was in the passenger seat, her hair blacker and shorter than Kate remembered. "Hi, Mam," she said, getting out and kissing her mother. She wore a red tunic, the bodice laced up with ribbon like a folk costume, and black trousers tucked into red boots. She opened the back door of the car and the child jumped out. He was small for six, pale and sandy haired, blinking, though the day was not particularly bright.

"Say hi to your granny," Emer said, and she pushed him forward.

Kate felt tears coming, and she hugged the child close and shut her eyes, so as not to confuse him. "Goodness," she said, stepping back to get a better look, "you're getting more and more like your uncle John." The boy stared at her blankly with huge gray-green eyes. She ruffled his hair. "You wouldn't remember him," she said. "He lives in Japan now. You were very small when you met him, just a baby."

The driver's door opened and the man got out. He was slight and sallow skinned, in a navy sports jacket and round dark-rimmed glasses. One foot dragged slightly as he came round the side of the car, plowing a shallow furrow in the gravel. Kate had been harboring a hope that he was the driver, that at any moment Emer would take out her purse and pay him, but he put a hand on her daughter's shoulder and she watched Emer turn her head to nuzzle his fingers. He was not quite twice her daughter's age, but he was close—late forties, she guessed. The cat had accompanied Kate outside and now it rubbed against her legs, its back arched, its tail working to and fro. Kate waited for her daughter to make the introductions, but Emer had turned her attention to Oisín, who was struggling with the zip of his hoodie. "Pavel," the man said, and, stepping forward, he shook her hand. Then he opened the boot and took out two suitcases.

"I'll give you a hand with those," Colman said, appearing at the front door. He wrested both cases from Pavel and carried them into the house, striding halfway down the hall before coming to a halt. He put the suitcases down beside the telephone table and stood with his hands in his pockets. The others stopped, too, forming a tentative circle at the bottom of the stairs.

"Oisín," Emer said, "say hello to your granddad. He's going to take you hunting in the forest."

The boy's eyes widened. "Bears?" he said.

"No bears," Colman said. "But we might get a fox or two."

Pavel shuffled his feet on the carpet. "Oh, Daddy," Emer said, as if she'd just remembered, "this is Pavel." Pavel held out a hand and Colman delayed for a second before taking it. "Pleased to meet you," he said, and he lifted the cases again. "I'll show you to your rooms."

Kate remained in the hall and watched them climb the

stairs, Colman in front, his steps long and rangy, the others following behind. Pavel was new, she thought; the child was shy with him, sticking close to his mother, one hand clutching the skirt of her tunic. Colman set a suitcase down outside Emer's bedroom. He pushed open the door, and from the foot of the stairs, Kate watched her daughter and grandson disappear into the garish, cluttered room, its walls hung with canvasses Emer had painted during her Goth phase. Colman carried the other suitcase to John's room. "And this is your room," she heard him say to Pavel, as she went into the kitchen to make tea.

"How long is he on the scene?" Colman said when he came back downstairs.

"Don't look at me like that," she said. "I don't know any more than you do."

He sat at the table, drumming his fingers on the oilcloth. "What class of a name is Pavel, anyway?" he said. "Is it eastern European or what? Is it Lithuanian? What is it?"

She debated taking out the china but, deciding it was old-fashioned, went for the pottery mugs instead. "I expect we'll hear later," she said, arranging biscuits on a plate.

"She shouldn't have landed him in on top of us like this, with no warning."

"No," she said, "she shouldn't have."

She found the plastic beaker she'd bought for their last visit. It was two Christmases ago, and the mug was decorated with puffy-chested robins and snowflakes. She polished it with a tea towel and put it on the table. "Every time

I see Oisín," she said, "he reminds me of John. Even when he was a small baby in his pram he looked like John. I must get down the photo album and show Emer."

Colman wasn't listening. "Are we supposed to ask about the other fellow at all now?" he said. "Or are we supposed to say nothing?"

Her eyelid was fluttering so fiercely she had to press her palm flat against her eye in an effort to still it. "If you mean Oisín's father," she said, "don't mention him, unless Emer mentions him first." She took her hand away from her face and saw her grandson standing in the doorway. "Oisín!" she said, and she went over, laid a hand on his soft, fine hair. "Come and have a biscuit." She offered the plate and watched him survey the contents, his fingers hovering above the biscuits but not quite touching. He finally selected a chocolate one shaped like a star. He took a small, careful bite and chewed slowly, eyeing her the way he had eyed the biscuits, making an assessment. She smiled. "Why don't you sit here and tell us all about the airplane?" She pulled out two chairs, one for the child, one for herself, but the boy went around the other side of the table and sat next to Colman.

He had finished the biscuit, and Colman pushed the plate closer to him. "Have another," he said. The boy chose again, more quickly this time. "Tell me," Colman said, "where's Pavel from?"

"Chelsea."

"What does he do?"

The boy shrugged, took another bite of biscuit.

"Colman," Kate said sharply, "would you see if there's some lemonade in the fridge?"

He looked at her the way the cat sometimes looked at her when she caught it sleeping on the sofa, a look at once both guilty and defiant, but he got up without saying anything and fetched the lemonade.

They heard footsteps on the stairs, and laughter, and Emer came into the kitchen with Pavel in tow. Opening the fridge, she took out a liter of milk and drank straight from the carton. She wiped her mouth with her hand and put the milk back. Pavel nodded to Kate and Colman—an easy, relaxed nod—but he didn't join them at the table. Instead, he went over to a window that looked out on the garden and the scrubland and forest beyond. "They're like gods, aren't they?" he said, pointing to the three wind turbines rotating slowly on the mountain. "I feel I should take them a few dead chickens—kill a goat or something."

His voice reminded Kate of a man who used to present a history program on the BBC, but with the barest hint of something else, something melodic, a slight lengthening of vowels. "Don't mention the war," she said. "Those things have caused no end of trouble."

"Perhaps not enough goats?" he said.

She smiled and was about to offer him tea, but Emer linked his arm. "We're going to the pub," she said. "Just for the one, we won't be long." She blew Oisín a kiss. "Be good for your granny and granddad," she said as they went out the door.

The boy sat quietly at the table, working his way through the biscuits. Kate remembered the board game she had found that morning and had left on the chair in the spare room. She thought about fetching it, but Pavel might notice it gone—would know she had been in the room in his absence. Oisín reached for another biscuit. "We could see if there are cartoons on television," she said. "Would you like that?"

Colman glared at her as if she had suggested sending the child down a mine. "Television will rot his brain," he said. He leaned in to the boy. "Tell you what," he said. "Why don't you and I go hunt those foxes?"

Immediately, the boy was climbing down off his chair, the biscuits and lemonade forgotten. "What will we do with the foxes when we catch them?" he said.

"We'll worry about that when it happens," Colman said. He turned to Kate. "You didn't want to come, did you?"

"No," she said. "It's okay. I'd better make a start on dinner." She walked with them to the back porch, watched them go down the garden and scale the fence at the end. The boy's hair snagged as he squeezed beneath the barbed wire, and she knew if she went to the fence now she would find silky white strands left behind, like the locks of wool left by lambs. Dropping into the field on the other side, they made their way across the scrub, through grass and briars

and wild saplings, Colman in front, the boy behind, almost
running to keep up. The grass was in the first rush of spring
growth. Come summer, it would be higher, higher than the
boy's head and blonder, as it turned, unharvested, to hay.
They reached the pile of timber that used to be the hut, and
Colman stopped, bent to take something from the ground.
He held it in the air with one hand, gesticulating with the
other, then gave it to the boy. Goodness knows what he was
showing the child, she thought, what rubbish they were picking up. Whatever the thing was, she saw the boy discard it
in the grass, and then they went onward, getting smaller and
smaller, until they disappeared into the forest. She moved
about the kitchen, preparing dinner, watering the geraniums
in their pots on the window. She rinsed the plastic tumbler
at the sink and watched the sky change above the Dennehys'
sheds, the familiar shifts of light that marked the passing of
the day.

An hour later her husband and grandson returned, clattering into the kitchen. Oisín's shoes and the ends of his trousers were covered in mud. He was carrying something, cra-
dling it to his chest, and when she went to help him off with
his shoes, she saw it was an animal skull. Colman went out
to the utility room and rummaged around in the cupboards,
knocking over pans and brushes, banging doors. "What are
you looking for?" she said, but he disappeared outside to the
yard. The boy remained in the kitchen, stroking the skull as

if it were a kitten. It was yellowy white and long nosed with a broad forehead.

Colman returned with a plastic bucket and a five-gallon drum of bleach. He took the skull from the boy and placed it in the bucket, poured the bleach on top until it reached the rim. The boy looked on in awe. "Now," Colman said, "that'll clean up nicely. Leave it a couple of days and you'll see how white it is."

"Look," the boy said, grabbing Kate's hand and dragging her over. "We found a dinosaur skull."

"A sheep, more likely," his grandfather said. "A sheep that got caught in wire. The dinosaurs were killed by a meteorite millions of years ago."

Kate peered into the bucket. Little black things, flies perhaps, had already detached themselves from the skull and were floating loose. There was green around the eye sockets, and veins of mud grained deep in the bone.

"What's a meteorite?" the boy said.

The front door opened and they heard Emer and Pavel coming down the hall. "The child doesn't know what a meteorite is," Colman said, when they entered the kitchen.

Emer rolled her eyes at her mother. She sniffed, and wrinkled her nose. "It smells like a hospital in here," she said.

Pavel dropped to his haunches beside the bucket. "What's this?" he said.

"It's a dinosaur skull," Oisín said.

"So it is," Pavel said.

Kate waited for her husband to contradict him, but Colman had settled into an armchair in the corner, holding a newspaper, chest height, in front of him. She looked down at the top of Pavel's head, noticed how his hair had the faintest suggestion of a curl, how a tuft went its own way at the back. The scent of his shampoo was sharp and sweet and spiced, like an orange pomander. She looked away, out to the garden, and saw that the evening was fading. "I'm going to get some herbs," she said, "before it's too dark," and, taking scissors and a basket, she went outside. She cut parsley first, then thyme, brushing away small insects that crept over her hands, scolding the cat when it thrust its head in the basket. Inside the house, someone switched on the lights. From the dusk of the garden, she watched figures move about the kitchen, a series of family tableaux framed by floral-curtained windows: now Colman and Oisín, now Oisín and Emer, sometimes Emer and Pavel. Every so often, she heard a sudden burst of laughter.

Back inside, she found Colman, Oisín, and Pavel gathered around a box on the table, an old cardboard Tayto box from beneath the stairs. She put the herbs in a colander by the sink and went over to the table. Overhead, water rattled through the house's antiquated pipes: the sound of Emer running a bath. From the box, Colman took dusty school reports, a metal truck with its front wheels missing, a tin of toy soldiers. "Aha!" he said. "I knew we kept it." He lifted out a long cylinder of paper and tapped it playfully against the top of Oisín's head. "I'm going to show you what a meteorite looks like," he said.

She watched as Colman unfurled the paper and laid it flat on the table. It curled back into itself, and he reached for a couple of books from a nearby shelf, positioning them at the top and bottom to hold it in place. It was a poster, four feet long and two feet wide. "This here," Colman said, "is the asteroid belt." He traced a circular pattern in the middle of the poster, and when he took away his hand, his fingertips were gray with dust.

Pavel moved aside to allow Kate a better view. She peered over her husband's shoulder into the vastness of space, a dazzling galaxy of stars and moons and dust. It was dizzying, the sheer scale of it: the unimaginable expanses of space and time, the vast, spinning universe. We are there, she thought. If only we could see ourselves, we are there, and so are the Dennehys, so is John in Japan. The poster had once hung in her son's bedroom. It was wrinkled, torn at the edges, but intact. She looked at the planets, pictured them spinning and turning all those years beneath the stairs, their moons in quiet orbit. She was reminded of a music box from childhood that she had happened upon years later in her mother's attic. She had undone the catch, lifted the lid, and, miraculously, the little ballerina had begun to turn, the netting of her skirt torn and yellowed, but her arms moving in time to the music nonetheless.

"This is our man," Colman said, pointing to the top left-hand corner. "This is the fellow that did for the dinosaurs." The boy was on tiptoe, gazing in wonder at the poster. He touched a finger to the thing Colman had indicated, a flaming ball of rock trailing dust and comets. "Did it only hit planet Earth?"

"Yes," his grandfather said. "Wasn't that enough?"

"So there could still be dinosaurs on other planets?"

"No," Colman said, at exactly the same time Pavel said, "Very likely."

The boy turned to Pavel. "Really?"

"I don't see why not," Pavel said. "There are millions of other galaxies and billions of other planets. I bet there are lots of other dinosaurs. Maybe lots of other people, too."

"Like aliens?" the boy said.

"Yes, aliens, if you want to call them that," Pavel said, "although they might be very like us."

Colman lifted the books from the ends of the poster, and it rolled back into itself with a slap of dust. He handed it to Oisín, then returned the rest of the things to the box, closing down the cardboard flaps. "Okay, sonny," he said. "Let's put this back under the stairs," and the boy followed him out of the kitchen, the poster tucked under his arm like a musket.

After dinner that evening, Kate refused all offers of help. She sent everyone to the sitting room to play cards while she cleared the table and took the dishes to the sink. Three red lights shone down from the mountain, the nighttime lights of the wind turbines, a warning to aircraft. She filled the sink with soapy water and watched the bubbles form psychedelic honeycombs, millions and millions of tiny domes, glittering on the dirty plates.

THAT NIGHT, THEIR FIRST to share a bed in almost a year, Colman undressed in front of her as if she wasn't there. He matter-of-factly removed his shirt and trousers, folded them on a chair, and put on his pajamas. She found herself appraising his body as she might a stranger's. Here, without the backdrop of forest and mountain, without the ax in his hand, she saw that he was old, saw the way the muscles of his legs had wasted, and the gray of his chest hair, but she was not repulsed by any of these things; she simply noted them. She got her nightdress from under her pillow and began to unbutton her blouse. On the third button, she found she could go no further and went out to the bathroom to undress there. Her figure had not entirely deserted her. Her breasts when she cupped them were shrunken, but she was slim, and her legs, which she'd always been proud of, were still shapely. Thus far, age had not delivered its estrangement of skin from bone; her thighs and stomach were firm, with none of the sagginess, the falling away, that sometimes happened. She had not suffered the collapse that befell other women, rendering them unrecognizable as the girls they had been in their youth; though perhaps that was yet to come, for she was still only fifty-two.

When she returned to the bedroom, Colman was reading a newspaper. She peeled back the duvet on her side and got into bed. He glanced in her direction but continued to read. It was quiet in the room, only the rattle of the newspaper, a dog barking somewhere on the mountain. She read a few pages of a novel but couldn't concentrate.

"I thought I might take the boy fishing tomorrow," he said.

She put down her book. "I don't know if that's a good idea," she said. "He's had a busy day today. I was thinking of driving to town, taking him to the cinema."

"He can go to the cinema in London."

"We'll see tomorrow," she said, and took up her book again.

Colman put away the newspaper and switched off the lamp on his side. He settled his head on the pillow, but immediately sat up again, plumping the pillow, turning it over, until he had it to his liking. She switched off the other lamp, lay there in the dark, careful where she placed her legs, her arms, readjusting to the space available to her. A door opened and closed, she heard footsteps on the landing, then another door, opening, closing. After a while she heard small, muffled noises, then a repetitive thudding, a headboard against a wall. The sound would be heard, too, in Emer's old bedroom, where the boy was now alone. She thought of him waking in the night among those peculiar paintings, dozens of ravens with elongated necks, strange hybrid creatures, half bird, half human. She imagined specks of paint coming loose, falling in a black ash upon the boy as he slept. Colman was curled away from her, facing the wall. She looked at him as the thudding grew louder. He was utterly quiet, so quiet she could barely discern the sound of his breathing, and she knew immediately he was awake, for throughout their marriage he had always been a noisy sleeper.

As soon as she reached the bottom of the stairs the next morning, she knew she was not the first up. It was as if someone else had cut through this air before her, had broken the invisible membrane that formed during the night. From the utility room, she heard the high, excited babble of the boy. He was in his pajamas, crouched beside the bucket of bleach, and beside him, in jeans and a shirt, his hair still wet from the shower, was Pavel. Oisín pointed excitedly to something in the bucket. In the pool of an eye socket, something was floating, something small and white and chubby.

Kate bent to take a look. Her arm brushed against Pavel's shoulder, but he did not move away, or shift position, and they remained like that, barely touching, staring into the bucket. The white thing was a maggot, its ridged belly white and bloated. Oisín looked from Pavel to Kate. "Can I pick it up?" he said.

"No!" they both said in unison, and Kate laughed. She felt her face redden and she straightened up, took a step back from the bucket. Pavel stood up, too, ran a hand through his wet hair. The boy continued to watch the maggot, mesmerized. He was so close that his breath created ripples, his fringe flopping forward over his face almost trailing in the bleach. "Okay," Kate said, "that's enough," and, taking him by the elbow, she lifted him gently to his feet.

"Can I take the skull out?" he said.

Pavel shrugged and glanced at Kate. He seemed downcast this morning, she thought, quieter in himself. She looked down at the skull, and at the debris that had floated free of it, and something about it, the emptiness, the lifelessness, appalled her, and suddenly she couldn't bear the idea of the boy's small hands touching it. "No," she said. "It's not ready yet. Maybe tomorrow."

Emer didn't appear for breakfast, and when finally she arrived downstairs, it was clear that there had been a row. She made a mug of coffee, and, draping one of her father's coats around her shoulders, went outside to drink it. She sat on the metal bench at the edge of the garden, smoking and talking on her phone. Every so often, she'd jump to her feet and pace up and down past the kitchen window, the phone to her ear, talking loudly. When she came back in, she didn't go into the kitchen, but called from the hall: "Get your coat, Oisín. We're going in the car."

Oisín and Pavel were at the table, playing with the contents of the Tayto box. The two-wheeled truck had been commandeered for a war effort involving the soldiers and a tower built from jigsaw pieces stacked one on top of the other. "I thought Oisín was staying with us," Kate said.

Emer shook her head. "Nope," she said. "He's coming with me. He likes galleries."

"I'll drive you," Pavel said quietly, getting up from the table.

"No, thank you. I can manage."

"You're not used to that car," he said. "I don't have to meet your friends, I can drop you off and collect you later."

"I'd rather walk," Emer said.

"Listen to her," Colman said, to no one in particular, "the great walker." He had a screwdriver and was taking apart a broken toaster, setting the pieces out on the floor beside his armchair. He put down the screwdriver, sighed, and stood up. "We'll go in my car," he said. He nodded to Oisín—"Come on, sonny"—and without saying more he left the kitchen. The boy immediately abandoned his game and trotted down the hall after his grandfather. Already he had adopted his walk, a comically exaggerated stride, his hands stuck deep in his pockets. Emer gave her mother a perfunctory kiss and followed them.

After they left, Pavel excused himself, saying he had work to do. "I'm afraid I'm poor company," he said. He went upstairs, and Kate busied herself with everyday jobs, feeding the cat, folding laundry, though she didn't vacuum in case it might disturb him. She wondered what he did for a living and imagined him first as an architect, then as an engineer of some sort. She put on her gardening gloves and took the waste outside for composting. The garden was a mess. Winter had left behind broken branches, pinecones, and other storm wreckage, the forest's creeping advance. She remembered how years ago a man had come selling aerial photographs door-to-door. He had shown her a photo of their house and, next to it, the forest. And she had been astonished to see that, from the air, the forest was a perfect rectangle, as if it had been drawn with a set square, all sharp angles and clean lines.

Noon passed, and the day moved into early afternoon. She listened for the sound of Pavel moving about the room overhead, but everything was quiet. Eventually, she went upstairs to see if he would like some lunch. She knocked and heard the creak of bedsprings, then footsteps crossing the floor. When he opened the door, she saw papers spread across the bed, black-and-white streetscapes with sections hatched in blue ink, and thought, Yes, an architect after all. "You could have used the dining room table," she said. "I didn't think."

"It's fine," he said. "I can work anywhere. I'm finished now anyway."

She had intended to ask if she could bring him up a sandwich, but instead heard herself say, "I'm going for a walk, if you'd like to join me."

"I'd love to," he said.

She put on her own boots and found a pair for him in the shed. They didn't take the shortcut through the field, but crossed the road at the end of the driveway and followed an old forestry path that skirted the scrub. Passing the pyre of timber that was once the hut, he said: "I saw your husband chopping firewood this morning. He's a remarkably fit man for his age."

"Yes," she said, "he was always strong."

"You must have been very young when you married."

"I was twenty-three," she said. "Hardly a child bride, but young by today's reckoning, I suppose."

They arrived at an opening into the forest. A sign forbidding guns and fires was nailed to a tree, half of the letters missing. He hesitated, and she walked on ahead, down a grassy path littered with pine needles. She slowed to allow him to catch up and they walked side by side, their boots sinking into the ground, soft from recent rain. Ducking now and again to avoid branches, they kept to the center path, looking left and right down long tunnels of trees. They stopped at a sack of household waste—nappies, eggshells, foil cartons—spilling over the forest floor.

"Who would do such a thing?" Pavel said.

"A local, most likely," she said. "They come here at night when they know they won't be seen." Pavel tried to gather the rubbish back into the bag, a hopelessly ineffective gesture, like a surgeon attempting to heap intestines back into a ruptured abdomen. When he stood up, his hands were covered in dirt and pine needles. She took a handkerchief from her coat pocket and handed it to him.

"Does it happen a lot?" he said.

"Only close to the entrance," she said. "People are lazy." He had finished with the handkerchief and seemed unsure what to do with it. "I don't want it back," she said, and, grinning, he put it in his own pocket.

It was quieter the farther in they went, fewer birds, the

occasional rustle of an unseen animal in the undergrowth. He talked about London and about his work, and she talked about moving from the city, the years when the children were young, John in Japan. She noticed his limp becoming more pronounced and slowed her pace.

"Thanks for going to such trouble with the room," he said.

"It was no trouble."

"I was touched by it," he said. "Especially the bear duvet and the rabbit."

She glanced at him, and saw that he was teasing. She laughed.

"She didn't tell you I was coming, did she?" he said.

"No, but it doesn't matter."

"I'm sorry it caused awkwardness," he said. "I know your husband is annoyed."

"He's annoyed with Emer," she said, "not with you. Anyway, it doesn't matter."

She sensed he was tiring, and when they came to a fallen tree, she sat on the trunk and he sat beside her. She tilted her head back and looked up. Here there was no sky, but there was light, and as it traveled down through the trees, it seemed to absorb hues of yellow and green. She saw the undersides of leaves, illuminated from above, and their tapestries of green and white veins. A colony of toadstools, brown puffballs, sprouted from the grass by her feet. Pavel nudged them with his boot. They released a cloud of pungent spores and, fascinated, he bent and prodded them with his finger until they released more. He got out his phone and took a photograph.

"I've seen Oisín three times in the last four years," she said. "Emer will take him back to London tomorrow, and I can't bear it."

He put the phone away and, reaching out, he took her hand. "I'm sorry," he said. "I don't understand why Emer would live anywhere else when she could live here. But then I guess I don't understand Emer."

"I'm a stranger to him," she said. "I'm his grandmother, and I'm a stranger. He'll grow up not knowing who I am."

"He already knows who you are. He'll remember."

"He'll remember that bloody skull in the bucket," she said bitterly.

Very softly, he began to stroke her palm with his thumb. She pulled her hand away and got up, stood with her back to him. Still facing away, she pointed to a dark corridor of trees that ran perpendicular to the main path. "That's a shortcut," she said. "It leads back down to the road. I remember it from years ago when the children were small."

This route was less used by walkers, tangled and over-grown, obstructed here and there by trees that leaned in a slant across the path, not quite fallen, resting against other trees. Ferns grew tall and curling, and the moss was inches thick on the tree trunks. In the quiet, she imagined she could hear the spines of leaves snapping as her boots pressed them into the mud. They walked with their hands by their sides, so close that if they hadn't been careful, they might have touched. The path brought them to an exit by the main road, and they walked back to the house in silence, arriving just as Colman's car pulled into the driveway.

They were all back: Colman, Emer, Oisín. Emer's mood had changed. Now she was full of the frenetic energy that often seized her, opening the drawers of the cabinet in the sitting room and spreading the contents all over the carpet, searching for a catalog from an old college exhibition. Oisín had a new toy truck his grandfather had bought him. It was almost identical to the truck from beneath the stairs, except this one had all its wheels. He sat on the kitchen floor and drove it back and forth over the tiles, making revving noises. Colman was subdued. He made a pot of tea, not his usual kind, but the lemon and ginger that Kate liked, and they sat together at the table.

"How did you get on with Captain Kirk?" he said.

"Fine," she said.

Emer came in from the sitting room, having found what she was looking for. She poured tea from the pot and stood looking out the window as she drank it. Pavel was at the end of the garden, taking photographs of the wind turbines. "Know what they remind me of?" Emer said. "Those bumblebees John used to catch in jars. He'd put one end of a stick through their bellies and the other end in the ground, and we'd watch their wings going like crazy."

"Emer!" Kate said. "They were always dead when he did that."

Emer turned from the window, gave a sharp little laugh.

"I forgot," she said. "Saint John, the Chosen One." She emptied what was left of her tea down the sink. "Trust me," she said. "The bees were alive. Or at least they were when he started."

Oisín got up from the floor and went over to his mother, the new truck in his hand. "If I don't take my laser gun, can I take this instead?" he said.

"Yes, yes," Emer said. "Now go see if you can find my lighter in the sitting room, will you?" She made shooing gestures with her hand.

The child stopped where he was, considering the truck. "Or maybe I'll take the gun, and I won't take my Legos," he said. "They probably have loads of Legos in Australia."

"Australia?" Kate said. She looked across the table at Colman, but he was staring into his cup, swirling dregs of tea around the bottom.

Emer sighed. "Sorry, Mam," she said. "I was going to tell you. It's not for ages anyway, not until summer."

IN BED THAT NIGHT, she began to cry. Colman switched on the lamp and rolled onto his side to face her. "You know what that girl's like," he said. "She's never lasted at anything yet. Australia will be no different."

"But how do you know?" she said, when she could manage to get the words out. "Maybe they'll stay there forever."

She buried her face in his shoulder. The smell of him, the feel of him, the way her body slotted around his, was as she remembered. She climbed onto him so that they lay length to length and, opening the buttons of his pajamas, she rested her head on the wiry hair of his chest. He patted her back awkwardly through her nightdress as she continued to cry. She kissed him, on his mouth, on his neck, and, undoing the remainder of the buttons, she stroked his stomach. He didn't respond, but neither did he object, and she slid her hand lower, under the waistband of his pajama bottoms. He stopped patting her back. Taking her gently by the wrist, he removed her hand and placed it by her side. Then he eased himself out from under her, and turned away toward the wall.

Her nightdress had slid up around her tummy and she tugged it down over her knees. She edged back across the mattress and lay very still, staring at the ceiling. The house was quiet, with none of the sounds of the previous night. She could hear Colman fumbling at his clothing, and when she glanced sideways, saw he was doing up his buttons. He switched off the lamp, and, after a while, perhaps half an hour, she heard snoring. She knew she should try to sleep, too, but couldn't. Tomorrow, they would return to London: Oisín, Emer, and Pavel. Oisín would probably want to take the skull with him. She pictured him waking early again, sneaking down to the bucket at first light. Swinging her legs over the side of the bed, she went downstairs in her bare feet.

A lamp on the telephone table, one of Colman's wooden lamps with a red shade, threw a rose-colored light over the hall. The cat rushed her ankles, mewling and rubbing against her. "What are you doing up?" she said, stooping to run her hand along its back. "Why aren't you in bed?" The door of the sitting room, where they kept the cat's basket, was partly open. She listened and thought she heard something stirring. The cat had been winding itself in and out around her legs, and now it made a quick foray into the room, came running out again, voicing small noises of complaint. She went to the door and, in the light filtering in from the hall, saw a shape on the sofa. It was Pavel with a rug over him, using one of the cushions as a pillow.

He sat up and reached for his glasses from the coffee table. He appeared confused, as if he had just woken, but she noticed how his expression changed when he realized it was her. "Kate," he said, and she was conscious, even in the semidarkness, of his eyes moving over the thin cotton of her nightdress. The house was completely still, and the cat had quieted, settling itself on the carpet by her feet. Pavel stared at her but said nothing more. They stayed like that, neither of them moving, and she understood that he was waiting, allowing her to decide. After a moment, she turned and walked down the hall to the kitchen, the cat padding after her.

In the utility room, she put on a pair of rubber gloves and, dipping her hand into the bucket, lifted out the skull. It dripped bleach onto the floor, and she got a towel and dried it off, wiping the rims of its eye sockets, the crevices of the jaws. She sat it on top of the washing machine and looked at it, and it returned her gaze with empty, cavernous eyes. Not bothering with a coat, she slipped her feet into Colman's Wellingtons and carried the bucket of bleach outside.

It was cold, hinting at late frost, and she shivered in her nightdress. In the field behind the house, the pile of newly chopped wood appeared almost white in the moonlight, and moonlight glinted on the galvanized roof of the Dennehys' shed and silvered the tops of the trees in the forest. She tipped the bucket over, spilling the bleach onto the ground. For a second it lay upon the surface, before gradually seeping away until only a flotsam of dead insects speckled the stones. Putting down the bucket, she gazed up at the night sky. There were stars, millions of them, the familiar constellations she had known since childhood. From this distance, they appeared cold and still and beautiful, but she had read somewhere that they were always moving, held together only by their own gravity. They were white-hot clouds of dust and gas, and the light, if you got close, would blind you.

ACKNOWLEDGMENTS

Thanks to: Kate Medina and Derrill Hagood and everyone at Random House for their faith in me and this collection; Declan Meade of The Stinging Fly Press, who first published this collection in Ireland, for his belief in and commitment to short stories, with thanks also to Thomas Morris and all the Stinging Fly team; Mark Richards, Lyndsey Ng, and all at John Murray, my UK publishers; Victoria Allen, for the wonderful cover design; the brilliant Lucy Luck at Aitken Alexander, whom I'm extremely fortunate to have as my agent; the Munster Literature Centre, especially Patrick Cotter and Jennifer Matthews; my writing group—Marie Gethins, Barbara Leahy, and Marie Murphy—who provided feedback with a stellar combination of brutal honesty and kindness; Lory Manrique-Hyland, for her workshops in 2010 and 2011; the Arts Council, for awarding me a bursary to work on this collection; Listowel Writers Week and Noelle Campbell-Sharpe, for my time spent writing at beautiful Cill Rialaig; Tessa Hadley and M. J. Hyland, at whose workshops parts of this book took shape; Cressida Leyshon and Deborah Treisman at *The New Yorker;* Anne Enright, Éilís Ní Dhuibhne, Ita Daly, Ethel Rohan, and Joe Melia, who provided encouragement in various ways; the journals, writing competitions, and websites who afforded my stories publication space and prizes; and all my writing friends, who have been so generous in their support.

Enormous thanks to John and our children, Ellie, Áine, and Rory, for things far too numerous to list here.

ABOUT THE AUTHOR

DANIELLE MCLAUGHLIN lives in County Cork, Ireland. Her stories have appeared in *The New Yorker, The Irish Times, The Stinging Fly,* and various anthologies. McLaughlin won the William Trevor/ Elizabeth Bowen International Short Story Competition in 2012. She has also won the Willesden Herald International Short Story Prize in 2013, the Merriman Short Story Competition in memory of Maeve Binchy, and the Dromineer Literary Festival short story competition in 2013.

@DanniLmc

ABOUT THE TYPE

This book was set in Caledonia, a typeface designed in 1939 by W. A. Dwiggins (1880–1956) for the Merganthaler Linotype Company. Its name is the ancient Roman term for Scotland, because the face was intended to have a Scottish-Roman flavor. Caledonia is considered to be a well-proportioned, businesslike face with little contrast between its thick and thin lines.